Next Summer

Dale P. Rhodes, Sr.

Jan-Carol Publishing, Inc
"every story needs a book"

Next Summer
Dale P. Rhodes, Sr.

Published February 2018
Little Creek Books
Imprint of Jan-Carol Publishing, Inc
All rights reserved
Copyright © 2018 by Dale P. Rhodes, Sr.

This is a work of fiction. Any resemblance to actual persons, either living or dead is entirely coincidental. All names, characters and events are the product of the author's imagination.

This book may not be reproduced in whole or part, in any matter whatsoever without written permission, with the exception of brief quotations within book reviews or articles.

ISBN: 978-1-945619-55-7
Library of Congress Control Number: 2018937793

You may contact the publisher:
Jan-Carol Publishing, Inc
PO Box 701
Johnson City, TN 37605
publisher@jancarolpublishing.com
jancarolpublishing.com

Acknowledgments

I would to thank my wife Phyllis for the unnumbered hours of listening to me as I teased her with little bits of the story as I was writing. You did not want to read it until it was complete. I hope the wait was worth it for you.

Thank you to our boys Dale Rhodes, Jr., Andrew Rhodes, Jeremy Bamburg and Zachary Pounsberry for your support.

Thank you to all the rest of my family who have been behind me all the way.

To those of my family who have gone on to be with the Lord, thank you for believing in and supporting me and I hope I have made you proud.

Thank you to Nikki DeRosa and Kelly Aylor for proofreading my manuscript and sharing in my excitement.

Thanks again to Mike Johnston for encouraging me to write. I hope you like this one too Mike.

Thanks to Spicy Penn for the use of your first name.

A special thanks to Da Juan Kenny for the gracious use of your first name and for being the inspiration for this book. I hope you like the story and your namesake.

Last but not least, thank you God for the gift of another story. I pray you will use it to be a blessing to others.

From the Author

In high school I wrote short stories in English class and poetry for myself. Poetry or my brand of poetry to be exact was a way for me to express my feelings and thoughts to myself if no one else. As dementia began to overtake my father and I saw the frustration he was suffering at the loss of a lifetime of memories slowly being taken from him, a stirring awakened me as well. As time passed he was unable to recognize us all, faces of his wife and children hidden from his consciousness. I hurt for him, I cried for him and I wrote for him. I watched my mother care for him. My family had encouraged me to continue writing and that soon became my first published work *Daddy's Apple Tree*. Time moves on. Life goes on. I have lost my father, my mother, my wife Erica, uncles and aunts and pets who have been more friend and family then I realized. All of those events have marked me and the many good and bad things in this life are what I draw from. I have been hurt and I have been healed. I know the old saying is that time heals all wounds. I personally think that it is life, life that hurts us and life that heals us. Life is what we make it and we are what life makes us.

My life had turned me from writing so when the idea of writing again came to me, I dismissed it very quickly. However this notion, this story of the guardian angel Thaniel from my first novel *If Only* would not be dismissed. For about three months, day after day this story simmered on a back burner of my mind and would not cool down. I talked with my wife Phyllis about this thought of writing a novel and publishing it and that I really did not want to pursue something that would require so much commitment. I truly felt however that the Lord had put the story in me for some purpose so we decided that I must pray and ask God what he wanted me to do. So I did, I prayed that God would help me and give me the story to write if indeed it was His will that I should do so. I told Him that I did not know anything about writing such a thing as detailed as a novel, even such a small one, but if He wanted me to then I would, if He would give me the story to write. As soon as I did this the words began to flood my heart and mind and I began to write them down. This second novel, *Next Summer*, is sort of a continuance of the first in that the same church is still alive and well and other members are finding their callings as well. This book was extremely fun to write and I hope it will be as fun or more to read.

Thank you for taking time from this busy, hectic life to read my work. I do hope you find yourself in it one place or many places. May God bless you for considering my work worthy of your time.

Sincerely,
Dale P. Rhodes, Sr.

Contents

Prologue – Friendship.	1
Chapter One – Office supplies at a time like this?	3
Chapter Two – No second chance to make a first impression	6
Chapter Three – Love and pranks make the world go 'round	9
Chapter Four – Finally, the first day of senior year is here	11
Chapter Five – There's no way we are backing down from a challenge	14
Chapter Six – There is nothing like that aha moment	18
Chapter Seven – Is there something you would like to share with the class?	21
Chapter Eight – What kind of caramel apple is this?	25
Chapter Nine – Some things are just not convenient	29
Chapter Ten – Plans are one thing, doing's another	32
Chapter Eleven – We gotta raise us some dough	36
Chapter Twelve – Laying on of the hands	40
Chapter Thirteen – First stop, butterflies or bad pizza?	43
Chapter Fourteen – Not exactly the big brother I had in mind	47
Chapter Fifteen – Now we are gettin' down to where the rubber meets the road	50
Chapter Sixteen – Pit stop, a little needed celebration	54
Chapter Seventeen – We are here to be a help	58
Chapter Eighteen – A little of this and a little of that	63
Chapter Nineteen – Now that's what I call a buffet line	66
Chapter Twenty – Taking it to the streets, preaching that is	69
Chapter Twenty One – Take up your cross and follow me	73
Chapter Twenty Two – Ah, the smell of lake water and pine trees	78
Chapter Twenty Three – A life well lived	83
Chapter Twenty Four – It takes a church to build a church	91
Chapter Twenty Five – Would you like an envelope for that	94
Chapter Twenty Six – What are we gonna do now?	100
Chapter Twenty Seven – Not another trip to the hospital	106
Chapter Twenty Eight – Memories aren't enough	109
Chapter Twenty Nine – What do condiments have to do with anything?	112
Chapter Thirty – That's a lot of sticky notes	116
Epilogue – Friendship in forty five thousand words or less	121

Prologue

Friendship

Friendship: Webster's 1828 Dictionary says that true friendship is a noble and virtuous attachment, springing from a pure source, a respect for worth or amiable qualities. I know, you're thinking *1828? Really?* I know, I know. And yes, there are many, much newer versions of dictionaries these days, but you have to admit that ol' Noah had a way with words. Friends make life easier. They make the good times sweeter, and the bad times bearable. The Bible tells of many friendships, but none like that of David and Jonathon. These two were such great friends that they loved each other more than brothers. That's a special thing, not something you see very often. It's almost unheard of today, but it does still exist. How can I be sure, you ask? Well, I'm sure because for the past five years I've witnessed it firsthand. That's where our story begins.

My name is Allison Parker, Allie for short. I am eighteen and freshly graduated. Bright-eyed and bushy-tailed, as my father says. I think I am a little more bright-eyed because of two boys I have known since we moved here, a little more than five years ago: Da Juan (pronounced dày-zhon) Noble and Sterling Silver. Yes really: *Sterling Silver*. Sterling is a nickname. His given name is Robert, but when he learned to read as a child, he turned a fork over and saw the words *sterling silver* on the back, and made the connection to his last name. So, this industrious young lad decided to nickname himself. His parents fought it for a while but they eventually gave in to it, as well as everyone else.

These two guys are the closest friends I have ever met. They are such good friends that they make everyone around them friendlier. I go to school...rather, *went* to school with a great group of kids, but we all have been held together by Da Juan and Sterling. I believe these two were des-

Next Summer

tined to be best friends, and to save us all from bored and secluded lives. Okay, I know what you're thinking: *Just what makes them such good friends?* I'm glad you asked, but to answer that question adequately, it would be best to go back a bit, and then maybe some more. So...

Chapter One

Office supplies, at a time like this?

This morning, the sun shines as brightly as the mischievous smile on Sterling's face as he steps out of his car and closes the door. His familiar energetic stride seems effortless as he walks across the parking lot and into the office supply store. Cheerfully he greets everyone else in the store, both customers and employees. Down through the aisles he goes, searching for the just the right thing. He catches a glimpse of Allison out of the corner of his eye. She is straightening some file folders on the next aisle over. His grin is so wide his face can barely hold it all, and the gleam in his eyes can only mean one thing. Allison has seen this look before. With a quick glance back to see where the manager is, she walks hurriedly to catch up with him.

"What are you up to?" Allison says, in that tone your mother uses when she catches you doing something naughty.

"Good morning to you as well, Allison. Why yes, it *is* a lovely day, and I am fine. Thank you so much for asking," Sterling responds in his usual confident voice as he comes to a stop in the aisle.

"Don't you try to use that stuff on *me*, Sterling. I know that look on your face. Now, *what* are you doing?"

"I'm just here in search of some much-needed office supplies, young worker lady, and yes, that *would* be very nice of you, to help me on my ever-so-important quest," Sterling says, in as cheesy a manner as he possibly can.

"No, Sterling. No, I'm not helping you with this one," she protests, shaking her head. Holding both hands out in a stopping gesture, she backs away a step. "It's too soon."

"It's never too soon for office supplies," he says, leaning in a little closer. "You *do* realize that your current line of work is predicated on your ability to help people find and purchase office supplies, don't you?"

Allison huffs at him and crosses her arms, shooting him a glare that would go right through him if eyes were weapons.

"What?" Sterling says, shrugging his shoulders. "Ooh, here they are." He points to the sticky notes on the shelf, then begins to look around for a basket. "Hey, where are the baskets?"

She rolls her eyes at him, then turns and walks away. He looks at another customer and smiles. "She's just a little testy today. I don't know why. It's a beautiful day, don't you think?" He says as he shrugs again. The lady just smiles back at him and shakes her head.

Allison walks back and holds her arm out, extending a basket to him as she comes to a quick and forceful stop beside him. "Here; now *what are you up to?*" she demands, a bit louder than she meant to. Several other shoppers turn to see what is going on. Sterling starts putting packs of sticky notes in the basket, pulling them off the rack in handfuls. Allison, embarrassed, whispers, "Sterling, for the love of everything good and holy, what are you doing?"

Whispering in return, Sterling replies, "I told you, I'm simply getting office supplies." He pulls the last bunch off the rack and drops them in the basket. "Do you have any more in the back? I already wiped out all the other stores in town."

Now totally frustrated, she hisses back at him, "*What? No*, and one thing I have learned over the years is that nothing is ever simple, when it comes to you."

"Oh, you're so sweet," Sterling retorts. He grabs her free hand and starts pulling her through the store. "Now, where are the markers?"

"Stop it! And let go of my hand," Allison fires back, jerking her hand free. "You're gonna get me fired."

"Here they are," he says cheerfully. He picks a multipack of markers off the hook. Tilting his head, he turns to Allison and asks, "Will these bleed through?"

Sighing and shaking her head, she takes the pack from him and looks at it for a second. Putting it back on the hook, she picks up a different pack. "Here, use these," she says, putting the new pack in the basket.

"Great!" he says, then pulls the rest of that brand off the pegboard display, letting them fall into the basket.

"He needs more time, Sterling. It's only been a few days," she pleads.

"Trust me, Allison. This is exactly what he needs," Sterling says, much more serious now. "I haven't forgotten what we just went through. What he just went through. This is my best friend. My boy. My partner in cr—well, you know, not *crime*, but everything mischievous that is considered legal." Now Sterling is smiling again. "This is what I would want, and I know it's what he wants. He needs to get back to normal as soon as possible."

"Okay," she concedes. "If you're sure about this... I hope you know what you're doing."

"Plus, how bad could it be? It's just sticky notes and markers. Ooh, I almost forgot: eight o'clock, my house. We have enough people, so it shouldn't take too long. See ya then, right?"

"Oh, no! I want nothing to do with this," she quickly replies, shaking her head and waving her hands back and forth in a warding-off gesture.

"Yeah, yeah, whatever. I'll see ya then," Sterling confidently says as he turns to leave.

Smiling and shaking her head, Allison whispers to herself, "Yeah, I'll see ya there."

Chapter Two

No second chance to make a first impression

As you can see, friendship—real, strong friendship—will make you do things that you really don't think you should, because you trust your friend. And yes, I plan to go to Sterling's house tonight to be a part of whatever hair-brained idea he has cooked up now. You know, it suddenly occurred to me that you don't understand why I have reservations about the whole thing. You see, Da Juan and Sterling have a great friendship, as I have told you, but what you don't know is that they are chronic pranksters, and they pull them on each other all the time. They love it. They thrive on it. Neither one gets mad, they just compete with each other, and laugh at each other and themselves. When they get bored of pranking each other, they team up and hunt for other prey. Ugh, it makes me shudder just thinking about the two of them against someone. They have been like that since the first day they met.

•••••••

13 years ago...

Saturday mornings are great. Saturday mornings in the summertime are even better. Saturday mornings in the summertime with a new neighbor moving in right next door, well, that could be great, or it could be a disaster that lasts for years. The sun comes up quietly this Saturday morning at the Noble house, but soon the quiet gives way to the sound of a large moving truck backing into the driveway next door. *Beep! Beep! Beep! Beep!* It seems as if the moving truck will never stop making that awful noise.

"Don't they know I'm trying to sleep?" Da Juan asks no one in particular, since he is in his bedroom alone. "Augh!" he screams out in frustration.

Thump-thump-thump-thump! Now, not only does he hear the beeping truck, he also hears his mother's thumping footsteps, coming to see what the screaming is about. "What's wrong, Da Juan? Are you hurt?" she asks, as she comes through his bedroom door, out of breath from panic and the run up the steps.

"That *noise*, Mom; I was trying to sleep," Da Juan whines.

"Child! You mean to tell me that you brought me up here with all that racket because you were awakened by a truck next door?" she scolds, standing with her hands on her hips and tapping one foot on the floor. "It's a good thing your father is already outside welcoming our new neighbors."

"New neighbors? Do they have any kids?" Da Juan perks up at the prospect of someone close by to play with.

"I do believe I saw a little boy about your age get out of the car that followed the truck," his mother replies, trying not to sound more excited than Da Juan. She really was excited, though. Ever since the doctor told her that she would not be able to have another child, she has hoped that he would find a good friend. "Why don't you get dressed and join your father while I get breakfast ready?" she suggests, as she walks out of his room.

Da Juan hurriedly throws on a t-shirt and shorts, then hurries to the door—but stops dead in his tracks before going out. Thinking for a few seconds, he dives into his closet, looking for something, tossing out everything that does not strike his fancy. "This will do nicely. Let's see what this kid is made of," he says, hiding his small treasure in his hand. With an evil grin on his face, he sprints out of his bedroom and rides the banister down to the front door. Without missing a beat, Da Juan leaps as he reaches the bottom and hits the floor, grabbing the door knob at the same time.

Just then Mrs. Noble calls out, "Da Juan, come here for a moment."

"Aww, Mom! Come on, you're killing me," he whines, as he turns and goes back into the house.

"You're OK Da Juan, calm down. I just want you to have your father invite the new neighbors over for breakfast this morning, please."

"Oh, OK. I will, Mom. Can I go now?" he pleads, itching to get out the door.

"Yes, go ahead," Mrs. Noble says with a little laugh.

He flies out the door and across the yard, running until he catches up with his father. "Oh, here is my son Da Juan now," Mr. Noble says. He motions towards the running ball of excitement heading his way. "Da Juan, this is the Silver family: Robert Sr., Laura, and their son Sterling," he says, motioning towards each of them respectively.

"Hi," Da Juan says, looking at the parents. Then he holds his hand out towards the boy, who reaches to shake it.

"Bzzz," The sound and vibrations come from the union of hands as Sterling cries out. "Aaargh!" He pulls his hand back, shaking it as he jumps back a step.

Da Juan laughs, a loud, proud laugh, as if he has done something truly spectacular—until his father gets involved.

"Da Juan, what are you doing? What's wrong with you?" he says, reaching out to grab Da Juan's hand. He opens his son's hand, revealing the trick buzzer. "You apologize right now, Mister. And give me that."

"I'm sorry," Da Juan says, pouting and looking down at the ground.

The Silvers all look on to see what is unfolding. Sterling steps forward to see the device. "What is that?" he asks in amazement.

"It's just a trick hand buzzer. It doesn't hurt."

Sterling, reaching to touch it in Mr. Nobles hand, says, "Can I hold it?"

Da Juan's father shrugs as he looks over at Sterling's parents. "Uh, yeah I guess."

The Silvers nod in approval as Sterling takes the toy and looks it over. "This is so cool!" Sterling says, then straps it over his finger. He holds his hand out to Da Juan, saying, "Now it's my turn."

Da Juan looks up at his father, to see if it's all right for him to engage in the handshake and sure punishment from his new neighbor. Raising his eyebrows and smiling, Joseph Noble nods his approval. Da Juan reaches out and lets Sterling get his revenge. "Aargh!" Da Juan screeches out, maybe just a little embellished to even the score for the day, and hold off any punishment from his father.

Sterling, smiling over the outcome says, "Cool! Do you have any more stuff like that?"

"Tons! C'mon, I'll show you," Da Juan replies.

Sterling now looks to his parents for approval. "Can I go?"

"Sure," they say in unison, and the two boys bolt away.

After a few steps, Da Juan remembers his mother's directive and stops quickly. "Hey, Dad; Mom says to invite the Silvers over for breakfast."

Chapter Three

Love and pranks make the world go 'round

Now you see how their epic friendship began. I think every epic friendship begins the same way, really. Not with some grand and noteworthy event, just a simple meeting. They just clicked, spending every day for the rest of that summer together. Da Juan and Sterling were inseparable. Campouts in the yard, sleepovers, anything and everything. If you saw one, you saw the other. It was one big, practical joke filled summer. Those two little boys loved to laugh, lived to laugh. It didn't matter if they laughed at someone else or themselves. The Nobles and Silvers had no choice in the matter. They were pulled into this bright, cheerful, fun, loyal, hopelessly contagious friendship. Their parents were the first victims—or rescues, depending on your point of view.

The pair pulled pranks on each other, then laughed and talked about what would make it funnier. There was the Friday night when they were nine years old, when Da Juan put shaving cream in Sterling's hand while he slept, then tickled his nose with a feather. Of course, Sterling retaliated the next weekend, by putting Da Juan's hand in a bowl of water while he slept, causing him to have to go to the bathroom so bad that when he woke up he didn't make it in time and wet his pants. Of course, there have been countless times when a frog was found in a lunch box, or a fake ice cube with a fly in it was dropped down into a glass of water. Once Sterling replaced Da Juan's lemonade with pure lemon juice. Not exactly the same.

Of course, for all the pranks and jokes, there have been an equal number of helping hands extended. From the loss of grandparents to the loss of pets, each time the two boys helped each other through the hard times. When sickness kept one from going to school, the other was always there to help him catch up on things. Even when the luck of the draw separated them onto two different little league teams, they still rooted for each other and practiced together all they could. It's always been like they were both arms belonging to the same body.

Okay, I know what you're probably thinking: *Enough already. Friendship, I get it. Let's move on, please.* Right? It's just so hard in the world these days to have something special that it's hard not to talk about it when you do.

Then came the first day of school. Suddenly, the rest of the world was fair game. Teachers have been especially vulnerable to their infectious smiles and humor. The playground is a great place to make friends, and the pair quickly became a small core group that has been together for a long time. Others have come and gone, moved here and moved away. Everyone who comes into contact with Da Juan and Sterling are changed, forever and for the better. They are always the center of attention, but they make you feel like *you* are. Everything is about being in balance and harmony, whether it's just the two of them or the entire group. They are the glue that holds everyone together.

Chapter Four

Finally, the first day of senior year is here

Ok, I get it, enough about friendship. Well, at least enough describing friendship. Why don't we get back to our story? You know, the reason we're talking at all starts back almost a year ago. It was the beginning of our senior year of high school. Kids in a Christian high school are just like any other kids, in at least one respect: If you're a senior in high school, you're top dog, El Capitan, the big kahuna, the...well, you get the idea. At least, that's how you feel. You know, kinda like Leo on the bow of the big ship, arms stretched wide, wind in his hair, nothing but open seas ahead. I mean, life is just about to begin, right? School is almost done, unless you go to college—but then it's because you want to, not because you have to. Soon, no one will be able to make you do anything, right? I mean, that *is* true, isn't it? We aren't just imagining things, are we? Good. I didn't think so.

So, there we were, fresh new school year ahead. So many things to do! Tests, quizzes, pop quizzes, exams, papers, projects... It's all really quite maddening. I mean, I'm getting a little dizzy just thinking back on it now. Spoiler alert! We did all graduate. No one was maimed, no one lost a digit, or anything like that. Sorry, I didn't want you be all worked for the rest of the book, wondering if I failed or not. Anyway, so there we were, just starting our senior year and already focused on the summer. Not even thinking about graduation: past that, all the way through to the next summer. Who does that? What's more, it was our teacher that encouraged that kind of thought pattern. I know. Who does that too, right?

········

Next Summer

Late summer heat continues as the doors to Pinnacle Christian Academy open for the start of a new year. Vehicles begin to pull up to the curb, and students find their way into the halls. Most of the children already know each other from church, so they haven't had a long summer apart. For those who don't go to church here, it is a time to reconnect with friends whom you haven't seen for several weeks. Pastor Richards, who doubles as the school principal, walks the halls and smiles as life is breathed back into the school. Many students come by to greet him—boys with the customary fist bump, holding firm to their masculinity, girls with a quick hug.

"Classes are outside today, right Pastor?" Da Juan says as he and Sterling walk up and double bear hug him, picking him up off the floor.

"Oof, he groans under the strength of their fierce embrace. They set him back down quickly. "You know, that's not a bad idea," he says, after he catches his breath. "We really need to look into something like that for next year."

"That hurts, Pastor. You know your two favorite students will be gone next year," Sterling whines in reply.

"Yeah, Dawg, that cut deep," Da Juan agrees.

"Oh, that's right; Allison and Kendra are graduating this year." Pastor Richards chuckles as the girls walk up to greet him next.

"That's so messed up," the boys cry out in unison.

"Girls rule. Guys, get used to it," Allison says as she hugs Pastor Richards.

The boys just stand with jaws dropped and eyes open wide as Kendra smiles an evil smile and joins in on Allison's hug.

"Pastor?" Sterling questions pitifully, his arms and eyes motioning to the two girls and the fact that they cut into their greeting.

"Relax, fellas," he says reassuringly. "We have a lot of fun things planned for this school year. I think you kids are in for a good one."

Hearing that, the boys jump in and form a group hug, shaking and twisting in excitement like puppies. The girls wiggle their way out, breaking the grip.

"Get *off* of us, you morons," Allison barks, and pushes Da Juan backwards into a locker.

Laughing and shaking his head, Pastor Richards waves them on to class. "You guys crack me up. Go on to class now, and have a great first day back."

Everyone scurries on to class to meet up with friends as still more students come to greet Pastor Richards. Mrs. Richards turns the corner, walking step for step with a young teacher who will also be enjoying his first day of school.

"Ah, good morning, Mr. Fisher," David holds out his hand as the pair approach. "I trust you are ready for the challenges of the day?"

Tim takes his hand, but pulls him in for a hug as well. "Brother Tim is fine,

Pastor. This all seems so weird, you know. Just a few years ago, I was walking these halls with books in my hands."

"Yes, well, he has a flair for the dramatic, doesn't he Tim?" Pearl chimes in as she gives Pastor Richards a look.

"I was just trying to be official and encouraging. All the things a pastor and principal should be," David says, trying to look contrite and a bit pitiful, but half smiling.

"It's OK, Dear. I was just being hard on you again," she replies, rubbing his shoulder.

"I'm so glad things haven't changed between you two while I was off at college," Tim says, smiling at the pair of comics. The sound of the class bell interrupts the conversation, but only briefly. "Well, I guess that's my cue. Off I go, to change lives and mold minds."

"Now who's being dramatic?" David speaks up, getting a chuckle from the other two.

"Yeah, I guess so," Tim replies, as he turns and heads toward his class room. After a few steps he turns back and says, "Even so, pray for me."

"That you'll do a good job?" Pearl asks.

"That they don't eat me," Tim jokes.

Chapter Five

There's no way we're backing down from a challenge

The class bell rings again, beginning the first period class as Mr. Fisher enters the class room. Chatter and laughter still fill the air, but slowly begin to lessen as everyone takes their seats. Those in the class who remember Tim from when he was in school and from church are smiling widely at him. Almost eerily, as if trying to unnerve him. He walks over to his desk to center his thoughts before he begins to speak. Looking up, he sees that now all of the students have the same creepy smile. Shaking his head, he can't help but laugh a little, which gets the whole class laughing (not that the kids needed a reason).

"I'm not sure if you guys are trying to ease my nerves, or creep me out," Tim says, still smiling. "Oddly enough, you seem to be doing a little of both. So, cut it out. Just kidding."

Da Juan speaks up. "You know we're just messing with ya."

"Yeah, brother Tim. You know us; Just having a good time," Sterling adds.

"Actually, it's good that you guys are my first class," Mr. Fisher replies. "OK, enough of that. Let's get going." Moving around to the front of his desk, he sits down on it and clears his throat. "For those of you who do not know me, my name is Mr. Fisher. I also don't mind Brother Tim if you like; either one will be OK. I do see that we have a couple of faces that I don't recognize, so why don't we go around the room and introduce ourselves? "

"Oh, man! Are you serious?" Sterling blurts out.

"No lie, dude. That's so cheesy. You sure you wanna start that way?" Da Juan tags in.

"Yes, I really think I do."

"OK, it's your career." Sterling tags back in.

"Leave him alone. Man, you two never stop. Don't worry about them, Mr. Fisher." Allison comes to his aid.

Several of the boys begin to cough out the words "teacher's pet." In response, she simply holds up her hand with the palm facing them and shakes her head.

"All right, that's enough fun for one day. Let's get things moving here," Mr. Fisher asserts. Allison begins and the whole class falls in line. Soon they come back to where they started.

"And I am Mr. Fisher. I used to be a student here, and for the last four years I have been away at college preparing for today," Tim concludes the roll call, and begins the work for the day. "So, you guys have just had summer vacation, and now here you are in history class." He pauses for just a moment. Then he continues, "I want to hear your thoughts. What is history?" Standing, he begins to pace back and forth in front of the desks. "What is history, and who makes it?" Mr. Fisher looks at the students as he talks. Coming to Da Juan, he points as if to pose the question to him, but just as he takes a breath to speak, Mr. Fisher interrupts. "No, not you. You two," he says, pointing at Da Juan and Sterling, "have had enough air time this morning. Let's give some others a chance."

Giggles erupt throughout the class, with a spritz of trash talk.

"Burn, baby, burn," comes from one corner of the room.

"Shot down in your prime, Dawg," from another.

"Ooh, gotcha," rings out next.

"All right, guys, it's not that bad," Mr. Fisher announces. "We'll swing back around to you fellas in a bit," he says, looking back at them. The boys look back and nod their heads as they grin at the commotion. "Let's get back to it now," Tim continues. Finding his way back to his desk, he sits down on it once again. "So, again, what is history? What is it for? Who makes it?" Looking out at the faces he lands on Kendra. "Kendra, what do you think?"

"Well, um...you know, it's what we do. I mean, everything we do. Everything everyone does," she replies.

"Tyler, what about you? What is history for?" Mr. Fisher asks.

Looking at his desk for inspiration and finding none, he answers, "So people can see what you've done. How you lived."

"All right, we're getting there. Bethany," he says. "What do think? Who makes history?"

Very chipper, she quickly answers, "Well, we all do. I mean, every day, right? Whatever we do becomes history."

"Exactly; now we're getting somewhere." Hopping down off the desk to pace back and forth in front of the class again, Mr. Fisher continues prodding the class. "So, if everything we do becomes history, and every one of us makes history, then what is history?"

"I don't know what you're trying to get us to, but it seems like something important," Raul says.

"I was wondering how long it would take someone to get that," Tim says as he claps his hands and points to Raul. "Very good. I *am* trying to get us somewhere. Think about this; history is made of two words."

Da Juan and Sterling finally break radio silence by sharing the connection with the class. "His," says Da Juan. "Story," Sterling finishes.

"Right." Mr. Fisher jumps up and points at the two boys, using both hands. "See, I told you we would come back around to you guys." He then walks over and fist bumps them both. "So, why is it *his* story, not *her* story?" Caleb raises his hand. Mr. Fisher quickly points to him and excitedly says, "Go, Caleb."

"Because in the English language, things that don't specify gender automatically are given the masculine."

Nodding his head, the teacher replies, walking around again slowly. "That's true, but I think it is something else, as well." Mr. Fisher is excited by the dialog and the class participation, so much so that he finds himself a bit jittery, as if on a caffeine high. To calm himself he stops and takes a deep breath, which gives the class the giggles. Smiling and a little embarrassed, he continues. "I submit to you that history is really in fact his story because it is *His* story, for us and about us," Mr. Fisher says, as he points up towards heaven.

Oohs echo across the class as Allison says, "So, our lives are God's story."

"Exactly. So, with that thought, what do we want our story for him to say? That's what I want to talk about first thing this year. I know, I know, maybe talking about what your life will be saying is a bit much for seventeen-year-olds. However..." he pauses to think for a moment. "Just think about next summer. That's not so bad, right? A very defined space of time. What will God's story for your life be for next summer?"

Everyone begins looking around the room at each other.

"Tough, isn't it?" Mr. Fisher asks. "And it only gets tougher, the older you get."

"Why do you say that?" Sterling asks

"Well, granted I'm only a few years older than you guys, but I can already see how fast life goes by. You all know that in the book of Matthew, the Lord gives the great commission."

"Go ye and preach the gospel to all nations," Jordan quotes.

"Exactly," Tim replies, nodding and pointing to her. "Well, as the years go by, you realize how short you have fallen of that goal. I know you guys are young, but I want to see you thinking about life goals as well as school and friendship goals. So, be thinking about this coming summer. You will all be graduated then—or at least I hope so." He quickly points to Da Juan and Sterling and smiles. They gasp and smile back, shaking their heads. "I'm not asking you to sign a contract or anything like that, stating what your summer will be. I just want to know you are thinking about life beyond this class room." Mr. Fisher pauses for a moment to let the challenge sink in. "Are there any questions or comments?"

Sterling raises his hand and as the teacher nods at him, he asks. "OK, so let me get this straight. All you want us to do is think?"

Finding his way back to his desk, Tim leans against it and replies, "Technically yes, but ideally, I would like you to think, pray, and let this be a challenge of sorts. You see, everywhere you go, everything you do, you are still a Christian. How the world looks at you—and for that matter, how other Christians look at you—says a lot about your history. The Great Commission says to go and preach. Now, not all of us can be preachers, but our lives can still preach. So, whether you actually do what you come up with or you don't, give it a good try." Tim looks over the class at the young faces, already showing the wheels of thought turning. "I just want to know that you are considering your life, your actions, and your words as a history that the world reads. So, what do you think? Give it two weeks, and we'll discuss this again, deal?"

Chapter Six

There is nothing like that aha moment

OK, so here we are, fresh out of summer break and ready to settle into a relaxing senior year—and the rookie teacher throws down the gauntlet. I mean, why would he do that? Why put the pressure on us of trying figure out what our legacy should be, when we aren't even old enough to have one? It's not just me, is it? I mean, really; think about it. Senior year! We are primed and ready to bask in the sunlight of all those underclassmen wishing they were us. We stand a little taller. Smile a little wider. We're at that special, magical time when we are not bogged down with the responsibilities of adulthood, but not looked at as kids, either. We simply float through the halls like we are invincible. Yeah, OK, maybe I did over-romanticize it, but you get the picture. So, how do you process a challenge of that magnitude? A challenge with long-lasting ripple effects that will go on long after you are gone?

Well, as you can imagine, we all thought about this throughout the rest of the day. In every class. In the halls. During lunch. At home. A lot of us talked it over with our parents for ideas. Some of us went straight to our knees and began to pray. Some of us decided to sleep on it. True to form, our social co-captains, our founding brothers, our spectacles waiting to explode at any moment in time took the only path that really made perfect sense. Da Juan and Sterling pondered it together. They did all the things that the rest of us did, they simply did them together. Scripture says a threefold cord is not quickly broken. I think they are as strong as a threefold cord without the third cord. I don't think it ever occurred to them to not do something together. They came back to school the following week with all of these ideas. Yeah, I know; we were supposed to take two weeks to work on it, but these guys were possessed or something. They couldn't wait another week. They had to get the teacher to open the floor for immediate discussion. You would have thought it was life or death, or something. It was like, "Ooh, ooh, can we talk some more about next summer? Please, please, please." It was kinda sickening, really, but the teacher loved their enthusiasm. The rest of us were just looking around, thinking "How do they always do this?" Then the two of them start this rapid-fire brainstorming session, going back and forth with all of these really good suggestions, like help out at the old folks' home; do fundraisers for a charity; car washes, dog walking, grass cutting, and babysitting. It was just a whirlwind of crazy energy. My mind is still in a blur just thinking about it. And of course, Mr. Fisher was like, "That's great. fellas. I hadn't considered a team effort." And then Da Juan was like, "I know, right?" And Sterling was like, "I know, awesome." And blah, blah, blah. Then more blah, blah, blah. It really was quite vexing. I mean, don't get me wrong; I love those guys, but *c'mon*. Of course, once I came to myself I realized they did us all a favor by suggesting we do a group thing. I just wish I had thought of it. Then, it dawned on me that we were not required to actually perform said actions, only to come up with good ideas. Then, of course, I felt like a heel for envying them. Don't ya hate it when that happens? Anyway, I digress. After the dust settled from the brainstorming tornado, Mr. Fisher told us to pass ideas around between us, and then we would bring the topic back up in another week. So, easy peasy, lemon squeezy, right? Our imaginary legacy producing project would be a group effort. The very next Sunday, however, brought an end to the imaginary portion of things.

•••••••

Pastor Richards steps up to the pulpit as the praise team winds down their last song. The auditorium is full of energy and excitement, as it usually is during praise and worship singing. The band members quietly sit their instruments down and the singers put their microphones on their stands. "Guys, thanks for the great music, and for helping to prepare us for the message," David says as he sets his Bible down on the podium. The band members all make their way down from the stage and out into the crowd to their seats. "Good morning everyone, and welcome the City on a Hill Church. I am so glad you decided to be here today," the pastor says, walking away from the podium. He looks towards the congregation. "I trust everyone is pumped and ready for the word of God this morning, so let's get right to it." Walking back in the other direction now, moving in front of the podium to make full use of the width of the pulpit, he continues his preface. "In a moment, we will have our scripture reading for our base text for today, but I want to give you the title I've chosen first. Just three little words sum up what I want to speak on: yesterday, today, and forever. Stopping his pacing and looking out across the stage at everyone he continues, "Now, I know you most likely think I'm referring to Jesus, but you'd be wrong. No, I'm talking about *you*," he says, pointing out at someone in the crowd. "And you, and you," he points at two more people. Walking behind the podium, he opens his Bible. "Now, open your Bibles, please, to the first chapter of the epistle to Timothy: chapter one, verse fifteen. Everyone please stand for the reading of God's word."

•••••••

"Okay, so now we can see how the Apostle Paul moved away from his bad yesterday and placed himself forever in the limelight, so to speak, as a Christian giant," Pastor Richards continues as he walks away from the podium once again, and this time sits down on the stage. "We all have a checkered past. Some are more checkered than others. The Apostle Paul called himself the chief of sinners because of his past. But God saw past all of that, and inspired him to preach the word; to write epistles; to travel on not one, or two, but *three* missionary journeys that spread the gospel like wildfire across the entire Mediterranean region. Paul left behind the atrocities of his past, and with God's help built a legacy that I would say is unmatched by anyone on this side of the cross."

Just as the words come out of the pastor's mouth, Da Juan and Sterling look at each other and then turn back to look at Allison, who is only a couple of rows back. The gleam in their eyes is instantly recognizable to Allison, who halfheartedly gives them two thumbs up, though she has no idea what scheme they have just come up with. Rolling her eyes, she puts her head down in her hands and gently shakes it, knowing that all in one fell swoop the wonder twins are going to change the lives of their whole graduating class—or at least their next summer.

Chapter Seven

Is there something you would like to share with the class?

I know, I know; I really need to work on my attitude. I'm usually not a sourpuss all the time. This whole event just seemed to get under my skin. And the fact that Da Juan and Sterling had such an easy time of it just irked me that much the more. I know what you're thinking, and yes, you're right. Instead of being envious because this, or everything, came so easy to them, I could have simply talked with them for ideas in hopes they would awaken something in me. You see, I am one of the last members to be in this group, so things don't always come to me naturally all the time yet. And don't be so critical, anyway! You know hindsight is always twenty-twenty. The important thing is that I see my faults and grow. Right? Right. So, getting back to the story...

This crazed look they had on their faces when they turned around and smiled, that "we've got this" smile, was just more than I could take. Especially when I had no idea what they had come up with, although clearly, they thought I should have. Of course, after the service was over, the pair of excited jackals nearly broke their necks jumping over the pews to get to me, to tell me the reason for their uncontrollable glee. After hearing their plan, I had to admit it was a good one. But I made them promise to give some of the others a chance to come up with something before they spring it on the class. They reluctantly agreed.

••••••

"Now that we are finished with our quiz," Mr. Fisher says, collecting the papers, "let's switch gears and revisit the discussion about our legacy summer." Making it back to his desk, he places the stack of quiz papers in the bin on his desk labeled *To Be Graded*. Being fresh out of college, Tim is full of vim and vigor towards teaching, and everything must be just so. Not that he was ever any other way; keeping things organized has always been one of his strong points.

Very eager to dig into the topic again, Da Juan speaks as he stands up. "So, Mr. Fisher, I..."

Just then, Allison turns her head and cuts him a hard look, reminding him of the terms of agreement they had reached the day before, stopping him silent in his tracks.

Looking up from placing the papers on his desk, Mr. Fisher replies. "Yes, Da Juan. What's on your mind?"

Feeling the heat from Allison's stare, Da Juan looks her way to see that she is not happy with his lack of patience.

"Go ahead Da Juan, what's up?" Mr. Fisher encourages.

Realizing that he has metaphorically stepped very far out onto a very short plank, Da Juan tries to paddle his way back to the safety of the ship. "Uh, uh..." is all that he can muster, however, as he looks back and forth between Allison and Mr. Fisher.

True to form, Sterling rises to come to his rescue. "Well, you see, Mr. Fisher," he says, sounding almost as unsure of himself as Da Juan, "we just wanted to say that we are excited. Yes, excited."

"Yes, *very* excited," Da Juan chimes in, as if he knows where Sterling is going with this. He glances over at his friend quickly in thanks, you, and then turns back to the teacher.

"Uh-hmm." Clearing his throat, Sterling continues, still a little shaky. "You know, to hear what everyone has come up with. For next summer." Proud to have gotten it all out without looking at Allison, who is still looking at him very sternly, Sterling smiles, which makes Da Juan smile as well, if only to seem all the more unified.

Mr. Fisher looks back and forth between Allison and the boys, sensing there is more to this story than he knows, judging from the kids' peculiar actions. He decides to let it go. "All right, then. You heard the man; what have you guys and girls come up with?"

After several of their classmates had spoken and exchanged ideas, the class became a bit quiet.

"Anyone else have an idea to share? You all really have done a great job with this. I want you to know that," Tim says. He walks around and leans against the front of his desk to continue his praises for them. "If you remember, I asked you guys to do this only as an exercise, to get you thinking about how you can be a benefit to others throughout your life. I simply used next summer as a way to bring the question a bit closer to home in your minds. Of course, you are not going to be graded on this, and I'm not going to hold you to any of these ideas. However, I won't discourage you from them, either. I just want you to see how we can influence others for Christ with sometimes the simplest of actions, as well as the great, planned-out projects." Noticing the fidgety way Da Juan and Sterling are sitting, he walks over to them. "You boys OK? Do you both need to go to the bathroom or something? Which would be a bit disconcerting, but whatever."

The boys both look over to Allison for approval to speak, which of course makes the teacher look over at her as well.

Allison rolls her eyes, half frustrated at them and half tickled that she has held such sway over them. Feeling the weight of Mr. Fisher's stare, she looks over to the boys as she sighs and then says begrudgingly, "Go ahead, children, go ahead."

Tripping over each other's words, they both cry out at once. "A mission trip! Let's take a mission trip. The whole class, and let's really do it, not just pretend."

"A mission trip, huh?" Tim says, running the idea through his mind. "To where? Or do I need to ask Allison this question?" he asks, smiling at her.

Allison's face turns beet red all at once as the whole class turns to look at her.

"I'm just kidding," Mr. Fisher says, still smiling at Allison. He turns back to the boys. "So, tell me more. Where do we go? What do we do? And most importantly, how does everyone else feel about this?"

"I was thinking we should go to several different places. You know, kinda like the Apostle Paul," Da Juan replies.

Sterling adds, very excited, "What about checking to see if there are towns in the US that have the same names as the towns that Paul went to on his journeys? We could go to those towns. You know, do what he did, but over here."

Raul joins in. "So, we could help each town with whatever they need help with, right?"

The whole class is now abuzz with excitement, and chatter fills the air. It seems everyone has already approved of this adventure, without even having it put to a vote. There isn't a single person in the room whose mind isn't going a mile a minute. So many new ideas are flooding in that the teacher has to quiet everyone again.

"OK, OK; let's all slow down a bit and quiet ourselves, so we can give everyone a chance to talk this thing out," Mr. Fisher says, his arms motioning downward like a quarterback trying to silence the crowd. "So, can I assume everyone wants to do this, before we go any further?" he asks, causing chatter to break out again like a rushing river bursting through a dam. "Well, all right then." He cautions, "This is going to take a good amount of planning. We need a team to start us off by searching for good candidates for towns to go to."

"Can we search for towns with the same names as the towns Paul went to?" Sterling asks.

"Yes, of course. I'd be very interested to know how many there are," Mr. Fisher replies.

Chapter Eight

What kind of caramel apple is this?

Well, in case you are wondering how many there are along with Mr. Fisher, the answer is not nearly as many as we had hoped for. It took a small group of us several days to search the internet for town and city names in America, and we could only find a handful. Out of the twenty or thirty-something cities that the Apostle Paul visited on his three missionary journeys, we could only find a few towns in America that had matching names. I know, I know; what difference does that make? The answer this time is it really makes no difference at all. We just thought it would be neat to try to set up a similar adventure, and that we could feel the same way he did or something. Have some grand connection to him through time and space. You know, travel to all these places, meet a bunch of people, do some good stuff. Tell people about God. Thing is, we aren't Paul. We are not supposed to have the same experience that he had, and neither are you. So, once we got over being bummed about the whole town names matching thing—or in this case, not matching—we realized it was time for us to have our own experience, not Paul's. Don't get me wrong, we all went back through the book of Acts and reread about Paul, Barnabas, Silas, Mark, Timothy, and all those guys to see just what they did and how it went for them. And of course, Mr. Fisher pointed out that along with doing good things and talking with folks about God, we needed to also include some preaching. We all quickly agreed that would be a good thing. The mission trip turned out to be the one thing we talked about in class every day. I mean, you know, we'd get our daily stuff done, but then we'd always find a way to get back to talking about it.

We soon realized that we needed to do a massive amount of planning to pull something like this off. I mean, first things first; where would we go? I'd like to tell you that all of us seniors took the reins and made it happen, but to be honest we were pretty much clueless. Well, not totally. We knew what we wanted to do, and when. We just needed help with the how. So, of course, it didn't take long for Pastor Richards to get involved. He decided we should start having a planning meeting every Sunday after church. I think he was afraid too much class time was being used for it. Maybe he was right. Not that anyone was in trouble with grades or anything like that, but I guess better safe than sorry, right? I don't know about the rest of the class, but I think I felt better when we started having real, serious discussions at church about the trip. I really liked the idea from the beginning. Don't tell Da Juan and Sterling, but as soon as they told me their idea, I knew we would actually do it. No need to swell their heads too much, right? I guess I just felt that if the whole church took our trip seriously, it must be a big deal. And that made me feel like we were doing the right thing, you know? Anyways, back to the planning. We split up. Some made calls all over the tri-state area to churches, to see who had things that we could help with. Some planned fundraisers so that we could pay our own way for this thing, and hopefully have some extra to help some people out along the way. Others started planning food for our trip and any other supplies we would need. Mr. Fisher was planning, as well. He and our youth pastor Jason Westwood began some serious praying for God to give us preaching messages for the journey. Still others felt that the school work and the work on the trip still left them unfulfilled, so they turned to planning more pranks. They shall remain nameless.

•••••••

Sterling feverishly fumbles through his bedroom closet, down on all fours. Clothes, books, old toys and a myriad of other things line his closet floor, making his search that much more difficult. "I know, I know; I need to clean up," he scoffs to himself, reprimanding and defending himself at the same time. Unable to find what he's looking for, he stands, scratching his head with a puzzled look on his face. "I don't get it. I've looked everywhere!" he exclaims to no one but himself, and continues his search. "It's like it sprouted legs and just walked off." Smiling and chuckling to himself, he continues his frustrated dialogue. "Maybe that's why Darwin thought fish had legs. He lost one, and just assumed it sprouted legs and walked away. Honestly, I crack myself up," he says, laughing louder now. Ready to surrender the backpack as lost, he switches to his best Shakespearean voice and dramatically proclaims, with his left arm reaching forward and grasping only air, "Alas, the time for rescuing is over, now I go forth conquering and to conquer." With that, he steps toward his bedroom door, reaching out for the knob. Closing his bedroom door, he reveals a coat hook on the back of the door—but his coat is not hanging on it. Sterling shakes his head as he sees that it is his missing backpack that hangs there. "If you're here, then where is my jacket?" he asks.

•••••••

"Da *Juan!*" Mrs. Noble cries out as she loads dishes into the dishwasher. "I see Sterling coming across the yard. Can you make sure the front door is unlocked for him?"

"Got it, Mom. Thanks," he replies. Running down the stairs, he jumps the last four and lands with a loud thud.

Mrs. Noble, startled by the sound, screams back to him, "Da Juan Noble! Is that really necessary?"

"Sorry," he yells back. "I'm just excited for tonight."

Honestly, she thinks to herself. *Those boys are the same as they were when they were five years old.*

Reaching the door first, Da Juan grabs the knob and turns it as he pulls the door open, quickly motioning for his friend to enter. "*Do* come in, Old Chap," he quips in a stiff British accent.

"Don't mind if I do, Old Boy," Sterling replies in kind. The two walk into the kitchen, where Mrs. Noble is finishing cleaning. "Hi, Mrs. Noble," Sterling says, setting his back pack on the counter, where he and Da Juan plan to prepare for the meeting tonight to discuss the trip.

"Hi, Sterling. Now you come over here, and give me my hug," she commands, motioning with both arms. Sterling walks around the kitchen island and reaches out for the hug as she pulls him in close. "There, that's better. Now, what are you boys up to tonight? And what's in the bag, Sterling?" she asks, with a puzzled look on her face.

"Well, you know, we need to make the caramel apples for the meeting tonight," he says quickly. Da Juan, however, is waving both hands for him not to mention the apples. Sterling now looks puzzled.

"Da Juan, I told you I had already made the apples for you. They're in the fridge," Mrs. Noble says as she turns around, almost in time to see him waving his arms.

Answering quickly but also a bit dumbfounded, Da Juan says, "Um, yeah; I know, Mom, but we, um…"

Next Summer

Sterling, now catching up to the conversation, tags himself back in. "Well, we...decided to make a few more, just in case."

"Just in case what?" Mrs. Noble ask, looking back and forth between the two of them.

Nervously Da Juan jumps back in to help his friend. "Uh, well, Mom, you never know. I mean, we may have more people show up, or everybody may be very hungry."

"So, we just wanted to have some more on hand," Sterling adds.

"Yeah, you know, just in case," Da Juan tags on with a smile.

Shaking her head, Mrs. Noble looks back and forth between the two of them. Assuming there is more to the story than she realizes, because there usually is, she decides to let it be. "I love you two, but sometimes, you're just weird," she declares, putting her arms up in the air as she walks between the pair and heads out of the kitchen. "You boys have at it, then," she says. "But clean up your mess, please." With that she leaves the kitchen and heads for the stairs.

"Whew." Sterling gasps as he finally exhales and relaxes.

"I know," Da Juan says, also relieved. "I thought she had us."

"Me too," says Sterling. "Maybe she's finally beginning to miss a step. So sad."

"Bound to happen sooner or later, right?" Da Juan giggles as the boys start to unload Sterling's bag.

"Oh...and boys!" Mrs. Noble calls out from halfway up the stairs.

They freeze in their tracks, afraid to find out what she wants. Looking at each other with terror in their eyes, they walk to the steps, stopping where they can see her.

"Let me know how the caramel onions go over with your friends. And for goodness' sake, give them the real ones after your prank," she says, proving once again that she can't be fooled.

Eyes wide, the boys look at each other and then at her without saying a word.

"How did I know?" she asks in a smug voice. "Sterling dear, onions don't smell through plastic bags near as much as they do canvas." With that, she smiles and winks, then turns and walks the rest of the way up the steps.

The boys, astonished, watch her all the way to her bedroom.

Chapter Nine

Some things are just not convenient

Yeah. Caramel onions. Real nice, huh? That's our wonderful friends. Oh... and how did it go over with us? Once we got the awful taste out of our mouths and wiped away all the tears, we chased them both out of the house. When we caught them—and yes, we did catch them—we dragged them to the back yard and took the water hose to them. We all took turns spraying the evil geniuses until we were all satisfied that their punishment was complete. Yes, and let me add that all four of the parents were watching through the patio door, and applauded us once we turned off the hose. Of course, we all bowed and curtsied. It was nice getting the tricksters back, but truthfully, I think they wanted to be caught.

I think sometimes a lot of people want to be caught. They don't always think of it that way, and may not admit it, but they do. Sometimes being caught is all they have going for them. When we planned our trip, we didn't know all the things that we would be doing. None of would have been so bold as to predict every outcome, either. We just knew that we wanted to do good and help folks, and leave the rest to God. That's certainly what happened in one town we went to. Sometimes when you try to help someone, there is a cost involved. We learned that the hard way trying to help one young man. But before we get to that, maybe I need to tell you a bit more about him.

•••••••

Next Summer

A little bell clangs above the convenience store door as another customer enters. The sound startles Russell, causing him to put the DVD he is holding back on the shelf. Sweating profusely, he backs away and walks around the store a little to calm his nerves. Just then, he feels a hand grip his neck, and hears a low rumbling voice in his right ear.

"What are you doing?" Smyth demands. "What's wrong with you? This is not that difficult. If you can't pull this one off, you'll never be able to handle the big ones," he says, still gripping Russell's neck tightly.

"I'll get it," Russell replies. "I just got a little nervous."

"Well, you better lose the nerves, Rookie. They'll either get you caught or get you dead."

"I know, I know. I can do it. It's just hard. I don't even *want* anything here."

"It doesn't matter if you want it, Moron. It's not about wanting it. Just do it. And hurry it up. I'm going to the car and if you ain't out in a few minutes, I'm leaving ya," Smyth growls.

"Hello, young man," another voice quietly says as Smyth walks out the door, ringing the bell once again. "Is everything OK? You seem a bit unnerved."

Russell, now totally distracted, turns his head to see an older man standing beside him. "What?" he asks, having not really registered the man's question.

"Are you all right? Is there anything I can help you with?" the man asks again as he holds out his hand for Russell to shake.

Russell looks this stranger up and down suspiciously before answering. "No. I'm doing OK, but you don't know me. Why would you wanna help me, anyway?" Figuring a hand shake couldn't hurt, he takes the man's hand.

"Why, indeed! Because it's the right thing to do, my young friend," the stranger says.

Taken aback by the comment, Russell thinks for a moment to himself, then responds, "My mother says that all the time."

"Well, she sounds like a smart lady."

"Yeah. I guess she is," Russell says, with a distant look in his eyes. "Well, Mister, I gotta go." He turns away and walks to the end of the aisle, then down the next. Finding something on the shelf that will make Smyth happy, he quietly slides it into his jacket pocket and coolly makes his way out the front door and into the waiting car outside. Climbing into the back seat, Russell pulls the stolen treasure from his jacket pocket and tosses it to the front seat beside Smyth. Defiantly he says, "There. Happy now?"

"If I didn't know better, I'd say you stole a backbone, Rookie," Smyth says, smirking. "Only don't stiffen it up too much around me. It'd be a shame for you to lose it, after you just got it."

"Whatever. I did what you wanted. That's all I know."

"Yeah, well, don't be getting' too cocky. You still have a ways to go. Oh yeah, and I don't know what you think you were doin' in there, talking to yourself like that. You're lucky you didn't attract attention to yourself with that stupid stunt," Smyth growls.

"What? Talking to myself? What are you talking about?" Russell questions.

"I saw you through the window, Dude. You looked stupid. Like you were having some great conversation, but with yourself."

Russell, thoroughly confused, doesn't know what to say.

"Yeah. You know, 'cuz you were by yourself," Smyth adds, looking at Russell and condemning him.

Pale, with a shocked look on his face, Russell sinks into the back seat of the car.

Smyth turns to look at him, shaking his head in disapproval. "Honestly, Dude, if you ain't up to this, then just tell me now. I'll drop your sorry hide back off at your momma's house, and you can let her take on a third job to support you."

"You shut up about my momma. She ain't got nothin' to do with this," Russell blurts out as he sits up straighter in his seat. "I'll do what you want, but leave her out of this." Russell now has his stare totally fixed on Smyth.

Feeling a bit nervous himself now, Smyth clears his throat before answering. "Yeah, whatever, Dude. I don't care anyways."

•••••••

Standing a ways off but looking into the car and listening to the conversation are guardian angels Haniel and his friend Jankiel.

"That was a perfect move, my friend, showing yourself only to Russell," Jankiel congratulates Haniel. "Also, nice using a comment that would remind him of his mother."

"Thank you, Jankiel," Haniel says, "but he still stole something from that store. I'm afraid I may need your help with this one. This Smyth character troubles me."

"Yes, I can see that. I will be right here, my friend."

Chapter Ten

Plans are one thing, doing's another

Just to be clear, that Smyth guy is not a good friend. I'm sure you figured that out by now though.

OK, enough about him. Let's get back to the trip. With everyone agreed on what we would do, it was time to start getting serious about the details. It took us several weeks to get a good list together of possible places to go. Deciding it would be better to make some sort of loop or something, so that our whole trip would be spent making the best use of time and travel, we drew a circle on the map and contacted more than 200 churches in the tri-state area. Sending emails and making phone calls, we asked questions about their plans for the next year. Many places don't plan a year in advance, but getting folks thinking about it was a good thing. Everyone we spoke with was excited about our trip and wanted to help us, if in no other way than to pray. We also asked if any of the churches knew of needs in their town that we could partner with them, and join in with the community to work on.

School days came and went. Tests and quizzes were taken, and book reports and projects were assigned and completed. We waited anxiously for responses from our questionnaire. We knew that these things take time, especially since we were asking for carefully thought-out responses, but it's still hard waiting. Wait, however, is just what we had to do. First semester ended, and we were still waiting. Homecoming came and went and we were still waiting. Thanksgiving finally arrived, and we decided to get together and play some flag football. That's when it happened: when we had finally let it slip from our thoughts.

•••••••

His bedroom window has a tinge of fog around the edges as Sterling wakes and looks outside. Rubbing his eyes and yawning, he can hardly believe what he sees. The ground is covered with white. That brightness wakes him up even more. Quickly he turns around and switches on his TV. Flipping through the channels, he lands on the local news morning show. After turning up the volume, he tosses the remote on his bed and starts digging through his closet. A moment later he backs out with his arms full of clothes, and drops everything on the floor in front of his bed. Looking over at the screen, he mimics the voice coming from the speakers. "And now the AccuWeather forecast, with Jenny Jasper."

"OK folks, we are going live now with Jenny Jasper, who is bundled up this morning, and it looks like it's a good thing she is. Is that a snow angel you're making, Jenny?" the news anchor asks.

"Yes, Skip, I am. You guys should be down here, it's a blast," Jenny replies as she stands up out of the snow. "Well folks, I told you yesterday that it was possible we might get the first snowfall of the season overnight, but to be honest with you, I didn't really think it was going to happen. Here it is, though," she says, arms spread wide open, motioning to the white blanket all around her. "We are only recording a few inches everywhere around the area, and it looks like tomorrow it will all be gone—but with a daytime high of only thirty-three degrees, today is going to be a fun in the snow day. Everyone enjoy, have some turkey, and be safe today. Most of all, be thankful, and have a happy Thanksgiving. Back to you in the studio."

As cheerful as anyone has ever been about the weather, Sterling lets his true joy come out. "Oh, Jenny Jasper, I think I love you! You always give me great forecasts, and you're so beautiful." With that he blows her a kiss, and puts on his snow clothes.

With a bounce in his step and a smile on his face, Sterling makes his way down the steps and looks in to see his mom cooking Thanksgiving dinner. "Morning, Mom," he says, then kisses her cheek.

"Good morning, Son. Did you see the snow? Or is that a silly question?" she asks, looking at his clothes.

"Yeah, I'm going out to mess in it for a bit. Unless you need my help."

"No, Dear, I'm on top of things. You go have some fun."

"Thanks, Mom," Sterling says, and turns to grab his coat at the front door. He steps outside into the brisk air and watches his breath rise in front of him.

The sun is bright and glistening across the four inches of snow in his front yard. Looking up at the clear blue sky, he takes a deep breath and dives into the thick white sheet, sinking to the bottom. The excited teen quickly flips to his back and begins making a snow angel, exhaling all the while. After a moment the angel wings come to rest, and Sterling reaches in his pocket for his cellphone. His now frozen fingers quickly search for his friend's number and tap the dial button.

Seemingly before the phone even rang, Da Juan answers. "I figured you'd be calling me soon."

"You see it, right? You see that my true love, Jenny Jasper, has come through for me again, don't you?" a gleeful Sterling asks.

"Dude, you do know that she didn't make it snow? Please tell me you do."

"Of course, but she told me it might. That's good enough."

"You gotta give it up, Bro. She's not gonna be your girl," Da Juan scolds.

"She could be. She's not too old. I just need to meet her, and it'll happen naturally," Sterling replies, smiling confidently.

"I love you, Bro, but you're delusional," Da Juan says, shaking his head.

"Anyway, when are you coming out to see the snow?"

"I'm—" Da Juan responds, but is cut off.

"It's magnificent. Gonna be great to play ball in."

"I know, I'm—" Sterling's voice is cut off again.

"Really, Dude, you need to get up and come on out."

"Sterling, I—"

"I'm just sayin'."

"Sterling, ca—"

"C'mon, Man! what are you waiting for?"

"Sterling! Sit up, and look to your left," Da Juan finally blurts out.

Sterling sits up and looks left as Da Juan says, and sees two long arms and his friend's familiar six-inch afro and smiling face looking back at him.

"Oh," Sterling says, surprised. "You making a snow angel too?"

"Of course. What else, Dude?"

• • • • • • •

The sounds of laughter and screams fill the thin air as the group of teens enjoy their football game. The whole group is here playing. They have spent most of their free time together for several weeks now, bonded much more closely by the desire to fulfill their new goal. But today is just for fun. A time to not think, to just breathe.

"Hut, hut," Raul says as he grasps the football between his hands, and the play begins. He takes a couple of steps backwards and surveys the field for an open target. Looking from side to side, he fires past the jumping Allison to get the pass away. Down the field, Sterling and Da Juan are running together, stride for stride. The two jump together, arms outstretched to reach the ball. It hits Sterling's hand, but he can't bring it in; arching into the air it goes. Coming up fast from behind, Joey dives and catches the ball just as he hits the snow-covered ground. Alert, he gets back up and begins to run towards the opposite goal with the intercepted ball.

Closing in on him fast, Kendra reaches out and grabs the flag on his right side as she screams out, "Gotcha!"

As the others are catching up to the action, Da Juan congratulates his teammate. "Good job, Bro." High fives spread through their team.

Just then, Allison says, "Wait! Hang on, guys."

Da Juan quickly protests. "No, no, no; that was a good play."

"No, I know it was," she replies. "Does everyone hear that? What is that sound?" She looks around, trying to find the source of her bewilderment.

"I don't hear anything," Sterling says.

"Quiet... I hear it. It's faint, but it sounds like..." Kendra turns towards the bleachers, where all of their bags are sitting. "It's coming from over there." She points to the bleachers.

"Is it our phones making that noise?" Da Juan asks.

Looking at each other, they begin to move towards the vibrating noise. "That's really weird, that everyone's phone would being going off at the same time, isn't it?" Joey contributes.

"You don't think something's wrong, do you?" Raul asks.

"Let's just see," Allison tells everyone.

"I got a bunch of emails suddenly."

"Yeah, me too."

"Me too."

"I did as well."

"Are anybody else's emails about next summer?" Allison asks.

"Yes," Kendra replies.

"Mine too."

"You guys know what this means, right?" Da Juan questions.

The whole group looks at each other for a moment. Then, with one voice, they all say, "We gotta get back to work."

Chapter Eleven

We gotta raise some dough

The emails started pouring in after that. Over the course of the next week, we received more than two hundred emails. Many of them were merely to say that they loved the idea, and wanted to contribute money, materials, or whatever else we may need. Also, many said that they appreciated us offering to help, but they had no major projects scheduled that they could not handle. Of the rest, we read and reread and discussed and re-discussed. Deciding where to go and what projects to be a part of is not an easy thing. Several churches were doing similar things, as well. It was pretty much unanimous among the lot of us that we needed to get other opinions, to help us break our list down to a doable size. After Mr. Fisher gave us his thoughts, we presented things to Pastor and Mrs. Richards.

Once the final list was put together, we reached out to all of the churches that contacted us. We found out quickly that it is not fun to turn someone down—but sometimes hard things have to be done, right? After disappointing some folks, we began to lay out the schedule for our trip to ten towns in ten weeks.

The only thing left to decide was how to fund the trip. Tony Edison offered to give us all we needed, which was great. That would have made things super easy, but after having a spirited debate, we decided that while we appreciated his offer, we really needed to do things ourselves. So, he made us promise him to let him help with any emergencies that we might encounter, which we did. The plan was to raise enough money to cover all our expenses, so that we were not a burden to the folks we were coming to help. If we had extra above that, we would use that to help them as well. Of course, the usual ideas for teen jobs came to mind: babysitting, dog walking, car washes, cutting grass, we did them all. But as I told you before, my friends Da Juan and Sterling are not your everyday guys. Sometimes, I wouldn't even call them normal. So, true to form, they came up with an idea that was so far out there that none of us, except the two of them, really wanted to do it. And yes, they guilted us all into compliance.

•••••••

Friday evening after school should be a great time, but on this Friday, it was pouring rain. All day long it poured; all evening it poured. Sterling lay on the couch in his living room, watching TV. Well, more like flipping through channels. His family had already eaten dinner. Mr. And Mrs. Silver made a family favorite to try to cheer up their son on an unusually quiet night for him: taco salad. Who couldn't get excited about taco salad?

Channel after channel he flips, sometimes watching for a few moments, sometimes flipping again right away. Boredom is a hard thing to break once it sets in. Sterling definitely has a bad case of it. After trying and failing to keep him engaged in conversation, his parents sit with him in front of the TV for a while. Around 8:30, Sterling decides he wants more taco salad, and asks his parents if they want some too.

"No thank you, Son. I've had quite enough," his mother says, and picks up the remote after he lays it down, smiling just a little as she does.

"Dad?" Sterling asks, looking at his father.

"You don't have to ask me twice," he answers, as he gets up from the couch. "I'll get the plates. You start unloading the fridge."

"Gotcha."

While they are gone, Mrs. Silver begins her own TV channel search, quickly landing on a documentary about Antarctic wildlife. Feeling both satisfied and a bit mischievous for stealing the remote, Mrs. Silver curls her feet up to the side and leans back on the couch, getting comfortable so she can enjoy the show. As father and son return with their overstuffed plates, Mrs. Silver looks over. "You know, it's not a competition to see who can get the most on their plate," she says. They both just smile, and sit down on either side of her.

Sterling suddenly notices that his mother has chosen an educational program, and voices his disapproval through a mouthful of taco salad. "Aww, Mom. Isn't there anything else on?"

"It's not going to hurt you to watch a learning program on a Friday night," she says sternly. "And don't talk with your mouth full. That's just rude."

After about thirty minutes of penguins, polar bears, and taco salad, Sterling gets a puzzled look on his face, He suddenly blurts out, "That's it!"

Mr. And Mrs. Silver both jump, startled by his outburst. "What in the world?" they say in unison, Mr. Silver barely holding on to his plate.

"Mom, you're a genius! Pure genius, I tell ya," Sterling says, looking at her as if she'd just discovered the missing link or something.

"Well, I don't like to toot my own horn, but since you said it..." she says facetiously, looking at her husband and shrugging.

"What is it that she is a genius about, Son?" Mr. Silver asks.

"Don't you see? That's what we need to do to *really* raise money! I gotta go call Da Juan."

"I thought you said he was at his cousin's house this weekend," his father objects.

"It can't wait. I have to call now," Da Juan replies, jumping up and running to his room.

His parents watch him run off, and look at each other in utter bewilderment. "Do you have any idea what that child is talking about?" Mrs. Silver asks.

"I was just trying not to lose my taco salad," her husband replies.

•••••••

"OK guys, Sterling says he has the best idea for fund raising you have ever heard of," Mr. Fisher says. "He calls it extreme fundraising, and claims that it will leave you breathless and exhilarated."

Sterling and Da Juan smile at the rest of the class and nod, feeling very sure of themselves.

"So, let's give him the floor and hear all about it," Mr. Fisher says, then takes a seat with the students. "How about you come up here, Sterling, and share with us all your master plan?"

Sterling walks up and stands in front of the teacher's desk. Smiling, he begins to speak. "OK," hey begins, hands held out as if he is about to catch a ball. "I know you guys are gonna think I'm nuts for suggesting this, but I really think it would get people's attention. Let me explain first how this idea came to me."

"Please keep it brief, Sterling," Mr. Fisher requests.

"Yeah, yeah, totally," he replies, nodding to the teacher. Turning his head back to the class as a whole, Sterling continues. "So, Friday night it was really raining hard, so I just sat and watched TV with Mom and Dad. And they made some super yummy taco salad."

"Sterling, *brief*, please."

Giggles emerge here and there throughout the class.

"Oh yeah, sorry. So, anyway, I was real bummed out and just flippin' through the channels when I decided to get some more taco salad. It was *so* good!"

"Dude, *c'mon*," Da Juan speaks up.

"I'm sorry, Bro, but I'm tellin' you they were epic. I had my plate mounded up like this," Sterling motions with his hands in the shape of a dome at least the size of a basketball.

"Sterling..." Mr. Fisher speaks up again.

The class is laughing all around now.

"I'm sorry, I'm sorry. OK, so anyway, my mom changed the channel on me while I was getting my taco salad. And she was watching the Antarctic wildlife show. You know, the penguins and polar bears and such. They were—"

Allison breaks in at this point. "No, Sterling. I know what's next. And I'm not doing that."

Da Juan is right on her heels. "Allison, why fight it? You know you're gonna give in."

"Give in to what?" Joey asks.

"Yeah, what are you guys talking about?" Kendra follows.

"But I've already talked to Jefferson Pools. They're gonna set one up for us, for the day. We can make a big event of it," Sterling says.

"Yeah, I understand. You wanna get sponsors and everything. I'm not doing it," Allison continues.

Mr. Fisher catches on, and begins to laugh.

"Don't encourage him, Mr. Fisher."

"What is it?!" the rest of the class yells out in unison.

"Polar bear! I want us to do a polar bear dive for donations," Sterling finally reveals.

"Ooh," the whole class says with a shiver.

"Yeah, *oh*. It's only *winter*; it's too cold for that," Allison pleads.

"OK, let's take a vote and see how many are up for it," Mr. Fisher says. "And if that's what you want, I'll do it with you—but I don't want anyone to feel forced to do it."

Chapter Twelve

Laying on of the hands

Well, I'm sure you know me well enough by now to know that I in fact did feel forced to be a member of the polar bear club. I suspect that you also know that I was the only one who did not want to do it. And most likely you have guessed that, despite all my reservations and pleadings, I did give in eventually, and joined the rest of the class and our teacher. What you may not have considered, however, is that afterward, I was glad I did it. The water was horribly, devastatingly, bitterly cold; it was the end of January, after all. The shorts and t-shirt that I wore gave no defense whatsoever against the frigid water that I submerged myself in, along with the rest of the circus that is my graduating class. I would never—and I do mean *never*—admit to the boys that I found it to be insanely exhilarating, and it made me feel more a part of this group than anything else I had done before. We all were shivering and laughing together. Of course, after a few short moments, we all exited the icy water and ran for warmth. The crowd that came to watch us, and many who did not, supported us well and we capped off our fund-raising campaign with this idiotic but incredibly crowd-pleasing event. After all the icy dust settled, we started finalizing our plans, and then focused on finishing our school year.

•••••••

"With that last name, all of our senior class has now graduated. Let's hear it for this exemplary group!" Pastor Richards exclaims, clapping his hands. Applause roars all over the stands of the basketball court, where the commencement exercise is being held. As the congratulations rain down on the graduates, their graduation caps go flying up into the rafters of the auditorium. Beach balls and confetti follow the caps, turning the room into a multicolored wonderland. The students jump and scream and bat at the flying balls. Pastor Richards lets the mayhem continue for several moments before raising his arms and asking for things to quiet down. "I am very glad so many have come out tonight to celebrate this wonderful accomplishment," he continues, once the floor is his again. "As I have touched on several times tonight, I believe this group of seniors is a special group. Not to take anything away from the students from any of our previous years, but this group has worked very hard all year, from the first day, to not only graduate, but to also plan for what comes next. I want to turn things over now to our youth pastor, Brother Jason Westwood."

Rising from a chair behind the podium, Jason walks towards the pastor, who meets him and shakes his hands, giving him the floor. Arriving at the microphone, Jason clears his throat and begins. "As teachers and faculty and even parents, we never really know exactly how far-reaching our words will be. Sometimes, they go far beyond what we expect or intend." Walking around in front of the podium, he begins to pace back and forth the entire length of the stage, microphone in hand. "I know most of you here know exactly where I'm going with this, but for the visitors, I want to continue my explanation. One of my former youth church members has returned this year for his first year as a teacher at our academy. On the first day of school, he wanted to share with our senior class what had been on his heart: namely, leaving a lasting impression on the world around him. Asking them to think about the same thing, his only real objective was to create an attitude of thought in his students. However, when the Holy Spirit gets involved with us and we surrender to Him, things can go far beyond where we intend."

Making his way back to the podium, Jason places the microphone back in its stand. "Ladies and gentlemen, our graduating senior class, your children, have researched, discussed, debated, planned, worked, called, emailed, and put their whole hearts into birthing this summer into a legacy to both grow on and leave behind. Shortly this group will leave here for a ten-week journey, to reach out and be a help to our neighboring towns and states. Contacting just over three hundred churches, they settled on ten places to visit that had great needs, and they are going to meet those needs head on. They have raised money to contribute financially to those needs, but on top of that, they will be putting their hands and hearts into loving and supporting folks in Jesus' name." Jason paused to look at the parents' proud faces.

"Their teacher, my student Tim Fisher, has been the best thing for this group this year. He challenged them, but more than that, he challenged himself. I believe they are all the better for it. Tim, myself, and my wife Renee are going to accompany the group on their trip. Together, with God's help, we are going to reach as many people and help with as many needs as we can."

Jason again takes the microphone in his hand and walks down from the stage as he continues. "Now, I would like to send our group off on a very high and unexpected note." Making his way down and stopping in front of the class. "I...we...myself, my wife, the pastor, and Miss Pearl, felt it was a good time to reward the hard work we have seen all year. When it was time to plan out our trip, and specifically the dates, I told the kids to leave this coming week open," he says, looking at the class and smiling. "Now, I told them they would need a few days to prepare themselves for the trip, which is true. I just didn't tell them how I planned for them to prepare." Walking around a bit more, he continues, "We had one church member in particular who has been very impressed by the determination of our group to earn money to pay for the trip. He wanted to contribute to something special for the kids." The while class begins to look around in excitement, and some light chatter breaks out. Continuing, Jason says, "To that end, we have a special week planned. Lord willing, we plan to take in a major-league baseball game, go to an amusement park, and see a bit of the city. After that, when everyone is all hyped up, we will hit the road and go to work." He sees the graduates are stunned by this news.

"Folks, I just want you all to know this has been a very special year for our school and our church, and I hope for all of our families, too. I know we are all proud of what we have seen these graduates do. Let's all please fill in around this group, and hold hands and pray for the Lord's blessing on all we are about to do this summer."

Chapter Thirteen

First stop butterflies, or bad pizza?

"Ungh... Ungh..." Allison hears the awful sounds as she walks down the hall towards the bathroom, lights coming on just as she needs them. "Nnooo..." The sounds of distress seem louder, but as if they are not meant to be. She has been awakened from her sleep by the overwhelming urge to go to the bathroom. As she turns the corner and reaches the girls' room door she pauses, but hears nothing. Thinking it odd, she wonders if by chance it was just weird noises from the building, and goes in to use the bathroom.

Everyone stayed the night after the commencement exercises so they could be ready to leave in the morning. Pizza, movies, video games, and just sitting around, talking and laughing meant a good time was had by all. Of course, everyone was up way too late.

As Allison washes her hands, she hears the strange noise again and jumps. "Ungh... Ungh... Looking in the mirror, her face turns pale. "What *is* that?" she says out loud, then covers her mouth so that whoever–or whatever–it is can't hear her. Instinctively, she reaches for her cellphone, but remembers she has no pockets in the shorts she is wearing, and that her phone is charging, anyway. "Ungh... "Ungh..." She could call and wake everyone or someone if only she had her phone but without it, what to do. She begins to look around the room for something, anything, to use to protect herself. Realizing there is nothing to use but her own hands, she stops and looks back to the mirror. "If that's Da Juan and Sterling messing with me, they are gonna wish they didn't," she says, this time loud enough to be heard but not caring. Her newfound courage in tow, she reaches for the door. Pulling it open slowly, she hears the awful noise again. Having let the door close again, she gets upset with herself. "All right, that's it!" she says opening the door again, this time with force. Allison hears the noise again. "That's coming from the boys' room. It's got to be those two clowns. I've had enough of this."

Ripping the boys room door open she yells, "What in the Sam hill is going *on* in here?"

Raul looks up from the floor and screams.

Allison screams back at him. Breathing heavily now, she takes a moment to compose herself before asking. "What are you doing down there?"

"Trying not to vomit," he weakly replies.

"Well, how's that working out for you so far?"

Looking back up at her as if no answer is necessary, he replies with a question. "What are you doing in the boys' bathroom?"

"I thought you were Da Juan and Sterling, pulling some lame joke."

"Well, I'm not. So..."

"Are you sick? Are you gonna make us all sick? Are you gonna ruin the trip?" she asks, not waiting for a reply before asking another question.

Trying to relax after the last dry heave, Raul answers, "Thanks for the concern."

"I'm sorry. I am concerned, but I mean come on, surely you can see why I asked," she says defensively.

"Yeah, I know." Raul looks haggard as he tries to sit up and lay his head against the wall. "I don't think I'm contagious. I think I just ate too much, or maybe there was something bad on one of my pieces of pizza."

"You sure? You're all sweaty, and you look like crap."

Raul just looks at her, clearly wanting to say something sarcastic.

"Let me go get Mr. Fisher. I'll be right back," Allison says, ignoring his expression and trying to seem more concerned.

"No, you can't do that!" he yells. "They'll make me stay here."

Allison looks at him with pity, but still thinks she should go.

"Please, Allison, you can't do that. I wanna go! I'll be all right. I just need to rest," Raul pleads.

Taking a deep breath and sighing, Allison sits down on the floor and leans against a stall door. "OK, how about I sit with you for a while, and see if you feel any better."

"Deal."

A few moments of silence later, Allison realizes she is actually relaxing in a boys' bathroom. Looking around, she gets a disgusted look on her face when her eyes land on the urinals. "They really are quite unnecessary, you know," she says, matter-of-factly.

"What?" Raul has no clue what she is means.

"Urinals. You don't need them. Why did they even have to be invented? They're disgusting. What, did the inventor think to himself, 'how wonderful it would be, to have a special way to pee that girls can't?' Did it make him feel like he had a leg up on us? You guys don't need 'em, you can do everything you need to do with a regular toilet. It's a wonder they don't just make them look like trees. Then you guys could pretend you're dogs or bears, or something"

"Yeah, OK... I didn't invent them, Allison."

"I'm just saying."

"As well intentioned as I'm sure you are, the urinal conversation is just making me nauseated again," Raul says, holding his stomach.

"I know, right?" she replies, somewhat happy that he seems to be agreeing.

•••••••

After another long silence and two hours later, Raul wakes to realize that they have fallen asleep in the bathroom together. Nudging her awake, he says. "Wake up; we need to get back in there with the others before they notice we're gone."

Waking and moving frantically, Allison jumps up, and they move quickly down the corridor to the gymnasium. Tiptoeing in between all the sleepers, Raul and Allison manage to get back in place and get a little more sleep before everyone wakes for breakfast.

•••••••

After breakfast, they all get themselves dressed and start loading into the bus. Amid all the chatter and laugher, Allison catches Raul looking her way and mouthing the words *thank you*". She smiles back at him, and he gets on the bus. Just as she is about to take a step toward the bus, a hand falls on her shoulder, stopping her. Turning to see who it is, she sees Renee Westwood.

"Yes, Allison. Thank you," Renee says with a knowing smile, and walks past Allison.

"Wait. You knew?" Allison squeals.

"Of course I knew. You kids may be able to keep things from Jason and Tim, but not from *me*, Sweetheart," Renee says, looking back with a smirk.

"But..."

"It's OK. I'm just glad he had a friend to sit with him. It is possible to be sick to your stomach without being sick enough to get everyone else sick. And look at him, he's fine."

"But how did you know?" Allison asks, catching up to Renee.

Leaning in close and putting her arm around Allison, Renee answers. "I had to go to the bathroom a time or two during the early morning hours myself. You guys are louder than you think."

Allison, totally surprised by the revelation, can't think of a word to say.

"I sat outside for a few moments and listened. When I knew you two were OK, I went back to bed."

"Thanks for not saying anything," Allison adds.

"My pleasure, Dear. It's nice to see how you help out your friends. You really are sort of the mother of the group. Now, let's go have some fun."

Chapter Fourteen

Not exactly the big brother I had in mind

Mother of the group? I don't know what to think about that. Is that like father of the bride? Do I get a movie deal out of this? That being said, who would play me? Who is the female equivalent of Steve Martin, anyway? Mother of the group—I just don't know if I like that or not. I wonder if it's just her that thinks I'm the mother of the group, or if all the teachers and staff think I am. Of course, now I'm gonna be paranoid about everything I do. I mean, I wouldn't want to do anything to tarnish the reputation I have as the mother of the group. Why would she say that? And is that a good thing to her, or bad? Now that you—I—mention it, she seemed a bit weird all the way around, didn't she? Who listens outside a bathroom door? And why was she up so much, going to the bathroom in the early morning hours? Did the pizza make her sick too? I'm gonna have to dig a little deeper on this one. I'll let you know what I find out, so stay tuned. Same bat time, same bat channel.

Anyway, speaking of mothers, I wonder what Smyth's mother thinks of his behavior lately. You remember Smyth, don't you? The bad influence, the rotten egg, the sour pickle? Well, I thought I would update you on him and young Russell. Smyth seems to have taken Russell on to be his latest project. You know, showing him the ropes, helping him get his feet wet. I don't think he's doing anything for Russell out of the kindness of his heart, though.

•••••••

"Why are you so hard on him?" Eric asks Smyth, with a touch of contempt

Next Summer

in his voice. "He's done everything you've asked him to."

Without even looking up from the photos on the computer, of a department store that he intends to rob, Smyth replies, "And if he continues to, then I'll let him keep hanging around. Mistakes will get you caught, Little Brother; you know that." Finally looking away from the screen, Smyth pushes his chair back from the desk and puts his feet up on it. "Look, I'm just trying to take care of you. If anybody is getting caught around here, it's gonna be the rookie. You *do* want to stay out of jail for a while, don't you?"

"Yeah, of course. I just wanna see him do OK. I mean, he's had a bad few years, ya know," Eric says.

"Look, I don't have anything against him, but he doesn't really seem like he wants to be doing this. He's way too skittish, and I'm not sure I can trust him. I've been doing this for way too long to let a rookie mess things up for me. I mean, for us," Smyth corrects himself.

"If you weren't always fussing at him, he might not be so skittish."

"Little Bro, I don't wanna fight with you," Smyth says, then shuts down his laptop. "When he gets back, just make sure he's got what I told him to get. That's all I got to say about him right now," Smyth grumbles, then walks out.

Left alone in the room, Eric sits dejectedly and contemplates the predicament he finds himself in. He has never felt good about doing what they do, but because of following his brother, he has never been without, either. Justification often comes from the thoughts that tell him they rob from rich people, that it's the only way he has to survive. He wishes his brother had never met Russell. It's difficult to watch another young guy be pulled into this kind of life. It is a very strong reminder that he himself was right there, in Russell's position, just a few short years ago. After sitting alone for a while, Eric drifts off to sleep in front of the TV. An afternoon nap is a regular thing for him, as Smyth goes off on his own often.

Knock, knock, knock. The sound reverberates off the metal apartment door. "Huh? What?" Eric mumbles as he wakes and rolls off the couch onto the floor. A short pause convinces him that he is hearing things. "Oh, man! I've gotta stop taking these naps in the afternoon. They make so sluggish," he tells himself, and stands up from the floor. *Knock, knock, knock.* "Okay, I know I heard it that time," he says, walking to the door. Wiping his eyes with one hand, he opens the door with the other.

"Good afternoon, Sir. I'm just out in the area today, inviting people to church." The clean-shaven, well-dressed man hands Eric a pamphlet.

A yawning, groggy, "What?" comes from Eric's mouth.

"My name is Jan. That's short for Jankiel, but that's neither here nor there," the man says joyfully. "Just wanted to invite you to church, and let you know that God loves you."

"He does, huh?" Smyth says, startling Eric. Brushing past Jankiel rudely, Smyth stomps into the apartment, grabbing the pamphlet out of Eric's hand. Quickly glancing at it, he tosses it to the floor. Without even looking back at the man, he says, "Not interested, hit the bricks." And with that, he slams the door behind him.

"Do you have to be rude to everyone?" Eric says to Smyth as he reaches for the doorknob.

"Just bein' honest, Bro. He needs to beat it. I don't need any goody two-shoes hangin' around."

Eric opens the door to see Jankiel just now turning around to leave. "I'm sorry, Sir; thank you for coming."

"You shouldn't do that. It'll encourage him," Smyth says as he walks across the floor. "And I don't want him back again. We heard enough of that junk when we were little kids."

A few moments later, Russell knocks on the door. He uses a special knock that Smyth has instructed him to use. Eric walks over and carefully opens the door, checking to make sure that it is Russell before fully opening it.

As Russell walks in past Eric, he sees the church invitation in his hand. "Where did you get that?"

"Did you get it? Did you get what I told you to get?" Smyth interrupts from across the room.

"Yeah, it's right here in my bag," Russell says. He lays the backpack down on the table.

Grabbing the bag and jerking it out of Russell's hand, Smyth begins to open it. He complains, "Took you long enough. I swear I could have built one, in the time it took you to steal this." Smyth takes the bag and goes to the next room.

Russell shakes his head and turns back to talk to Eric. "So, where did you get that paper?"

"Some guy knocked on the door and handed it to me. He said God loves me."

"That's so strange."

"Why do you say that?"

"As I was walking over here, just a couple of blocks away, a gust of wind came up out of nowhere and this blew up off the sidewalk and hit me in the face," Russell replies, pulling another church invitation from his pocket.

"You two choir boys wanna stop wasting time and come help me set up for the next job?" Smyth grumbles as he walks back into the room.

Chapter Fifteen

Now we're gettin' to where the rubber meets the road

After a few hours in the city, the church bus finally reaches the stadium parking lot. Everyone is excited to see the game. They all unload, laughing and joking, and file in with the thousands of others funneling through the gates and the many metal detectors. Once inside, the adults make a mad dash to find the nearest restrooms while the kids laugh at them. Renee, upon exiting the ladies room and meeting back up with the group, laughingly warns them all that they will be in her shoes in fifteen years or so. An appropriate number of t-shirts and foam fingers are purchased, and everyone makes it to their seat in time for the national anthem. Just as it is ending, the whole group looks at one another, and in unison they scream out, "Play ball!"

•••••••

Tom Hanks made us all aware of the fact that there is no crying in baseball. What he did not tell us, or maybe I wasn't listening all that well, is that there is a lot of real life in baseball. You have one on one battles between the batter and the pitcher. That's sort of like David versus Goliath. Then there is team against team, which is like nation against nation. You have the secret codes of war given by the third base coach, which is really ingenious, because most of those crazy signs mean nothing. There is victory and defeat. In the playoffs, there is life and death; well, not real life, but baseball life. Of course, winning a championship is that mountain-top experience that we all want, no matter what we do in life.

I think you can also learn a lot about your friends by going to a game with them. Maybe not everyone is a sports fan, but it's nice when you can go as a group and just have a good time and enjoy the experience. You get to see the craziness of the fans close up. The painted faces and the accessories some of these people wear make it like going to a costume party. I watched my friend Raul, who is usually one of these guys who can eat as much as he wants of whatever he wants, being very cautious about what he ate at the game, after the pizza the night before. I could tell that he wanted to pig out, but he was afraid to. Then there's Joey, who is usually a very quiet guy—but he is a baseball freak, so at the stadium he is in paradise. Screaming, arguing over the calls, jumping up and down, he loves it all. Of course, he has to have a stadium dog in his hand throughout the entire game. I don't know where he puts it all. Guys are so lucky. Mr. Fisher loves baseball too, so the two of them were joined at the hip all afternoon. Kendra is a people watcher. She doesn't care about baseball one way or the other, but having that many people in one place to study, her brain goes into overload. I bet she will become a detective or something. She sees everything. Speaking of future careers, I have always assumed that Da Juan would one day be president, and Sterling his vice president. Then I figure they will switch, if that's even allowed. They just do everything well. It's like they are born naturals at whatever they try. Me, I just like to see happiness and peace. Wow, that sounded better in my head. I feel like I just finished an interview for the Miss America pageant. OK, moving on, that brings us to Jason and Renee. As you may know, they both have had much pain in their lives, so they seem to thrive on the excitement of surprise. They are always leaving each other cards and little gifts and such. They love anything that will bring a smile to the other's face. And that, my friend, is where I will put you back into the story.

•••••••

"That's three outs, folks, and that means it's time for the seventh-inning stretch!" the stadium announcer proclaims.

"I'm going back for another hot dog," Joey declares, rising from his seat.

"No, you can't," Kendra says, as she grabs his forearm. "Remember, Renee said she wanted us all to stay put for the seventh-inning stretch."

"Oh yeah, I forgot." He sits back down.

"Ladies and gentlemen, please rise and reach for the sky. Let's get a good stretch and loosen up your singing voice. It's time for 'Take Me Out to the Ball Game,'" the announcer says as the music starts. "OK, are you ready? Are you ready? Let's go! Take me out to the ballgame..." The announcer gets the song going, and the crowd joins in. On the big screen, you can see happy fans singing, babies sleeping, and fans in line at the concession stands.

As the song comes to an end, the stadium erupts in cheering and clapping hands. "I don't understand why Renee wanted us to stay here for the song. They do it all the time," Allison says to Kendra, whose reply is simply a shrug.

The stadium announcer comes back to continue the stretch. "All right folks, that was great singing. We have some special guests with us tonight. All this past school year, a group of high school seniors have been planning a mission trip around our area, to lend a hand and do some great things. They're heading out in a couple of days, and are here celebrating with us tonight." The big screen now shows that the cameras are all pointed at the group. The kids are all shocked, but recover quickly and start screaming and jumping up and down. "Folks, let's have a big round of applause for this year's graduating class from Pinnacle Christian School." With that, the whole stadium erupts with cheers and clapping again. "And in honor of all the good they're gonna do for our area, let's sing one more song." The music for "God Bless America" begins, and the announcer starts off the singing again. "OK folks. You all know this one, too. Join in with me, let's go. God bless America..." The kids are all singing and clapping by his second word. As the song comes to an end, they all gather around Renee and have a group hug.

"Thank you, Pinnacle Christian Warriors. Go get 'em! Now, I know this has been a long stretch, but we have one more surprise tonight, folks." The announcer continues, "We love to share in our fans' joys here at the park, and tonight there is one special fan whose wife has a wonderful surprise for him. Folks, tonight we have a young couple whose family is about to begin. Yep, there is a young lady with us who wants to surprise her husband tonight by letting him know that she is pregnant with their first child." Again, cheering breaks out throughout the stadium. "Okay folks, why don't we start the wave as the cameras move throughout the crowd, searching for that lucky fan?" the announcer requests.

The wave starts; whole sections of fans rise and raise their hands and then sit back down. Cameras focus on the fans throughout the stadium, and different couples are shown on the big screen. "Is it *this* couple?" the announcer asks, as a couple shows up on the screen. The husband looks at his wife, and she shakes her head. The announcer keeps moving as different couples show up on the screen.

"I love this kind of stuff," Jason says as he nudges Tim with an elbow. "I think it's a great way to surprise someone you love."

"Yeah, it's pretty cool," Tim leans over to say.

"How about this couple?" the announcer asks, as Renee and Jason show up on the big screen.

"Hey, Jason, it's you and Renee on the screen," Tim says, and points to the screen behind the center field wall.

"Oh yeah," Jason says. Then he turns to Renee. "Look, Honey, it's us."

"Yeah, what do you think?" Renee answers.

"Well, what do you think folks? Is it *this* couple?" the announcer asks again. The crowd suddenly gets quiet.

"Think about what, Dear?" Jason asks, with a puzzled look on his face.

"Think about being a father, silly," Renee says. She points to Jason and starts nodding while turning to face the camera.

"Looks like we have a winner, folks," the announcer says. The crowd goes crazy with cheers and applause. "That's right, folks! This is Jason and Renee Westwood, and Jason, your wife Renee wants you to know that she is pregnant. You are gonna be a dad!"

"What?" Jason says, totally surprised. He looks at Renee for confirmation.

Nodding again and smiling, she replies, "Yes, Dear; you're gonna be a dad."

Jason wraps his arms around Renee, lifting her off the floor and hugging her. Putting her back down, he kisses her and says, "Wow, what a great surprise! You got me good. I love you, Sweetheart."

"I love you too," she says.

"Congratulations, Jason and Renee, and thanks for sharing such a wonderful moment with us here at the park. OK folks, let's get back to baseball."

As the team heads back out onto the field, Allison leans over towards Kendra and says, "I thought she was acting funny this morning, but I never saw this coming."

"Why, what did she do?" Kendra asks.

"Long story, I'll tell ya later."

The group all gathers around Jason and Renee to pat them on the back and hug them. Congratulations come from all directions.

Chapter Sixteen

Making a pit stop for a little needed celebration

She's pregnant! Now it all makes perfect sense. I kept thinking about it all day; how did she hear us from the gymnasium? Did we wake her? Is that why she was up using the bathroom, or did the pizza make her sick, too? Was she just paranoid to have that many teenagers together for a sleepover, and couldn't sleep? The whole morning, all these questions ran through my mind. Mostly, I was just glad that she didn't make Raul stay home. That was pretty cool of her. I guess technically, she could've made him go to the doctor, but I'm glad she didn't. Incidentally, Raul was fine. Like I said, he took it easy on the ballpark food, but after that he was good to go. Isn't that funny? So many others ate the same pizza, and no one else got sick like that. It seemingly makes no sense, but I guess there's a lot of things that go on inside us that we aren't even aware of. So, she's pregnant. I told you they like to surprise each other. They do it all the time. It's their sort of thing, trying to surprise the other, better. I guess it's kinda cute.

So, we had a pretty good week. We saw an off-Broadway play, caught a baseball game, had a blast at the amusement park, and hung out in the city some as well. Crowds cheered for us at the game, and we found out Jason and Renee are gonna have a baby. Pretty amazing start to our summer, I would say.

And then it happened.

·······

Boom, boom, boom, crack, crack, boom! The terrible sounds shook the hotel room, vibrating the windows. "What on earth is that?" Sterling asks, almost jumping out of his bed.

"It's just thunder, Dude. Go back to sleep," Da Juan replies. "It's not time to get up. It's only five thirty."

"Oh, all right. Goodnight."

"Goodnight."

"Again."

"What?"

"I mean, I guess it's really good morning, but I'm going back to sleep."

"OK, good morning or night, whatever."

"I mean, I'm just saying."

"Sterling. Dude. Go back to sleep."

The boys cannot hold their eyes open any longer and drift off.

Knocking at the door beckons the boys to wake up.

"Sterling, get the door, Dude, please," Da Juan pleads, covering his head with the sheet.

Knock, knock, knock.

"*Again* with the knocking?" Da Juan whines.

"I got it, Bro," Sterling assures, him slowly slipping out of the bed. Fumbling his way to the door, he arrives just in time to hear the third batch of knocks. "OK, OK! I'm here," he says as he looks through the little glass peephole. Turning the lock, he calls out, "Joey, what do want with us at five thirty in the morning?" He opens the door to see Joey's puzzled look.

"It's not five thirty, guys. It's *eight* thirty."

"I thought you said it was five thirty, Bro," Sterling says as he turns to face Da Juan.

Uncovering his head and reluctantly looking up to face his friends, Da Juan answers, "I'm tellin' you, you woke up because of the thunder, and I looked at the clock, and it was five thirty."

"It stopped storming over an hour ago." Joey broke the news to them.

"So, what you're saying is that we slept three hours, and it felt like a blink of an eye?" Sterling says.

"I'm afraid so, guys. Sorry," Joey says, apologetically.

The two look at each other and then at the window, where they see a light glowing behind the drawn curtains. Da Juan covers his head. Sterling walks back over to his bed and falls face first back onto it.

"Anyway, we are all gathering for breakfast downstairs," Joey offers, hoping the mention of food will cheer his friends.

Both boys mumble into their sheets that they will be down soon.

••••••

Da Juan and Sterling make their way off the elevators and into the hallway leading to the dining room. Noticing that everything is dark and quiet, Sterling speaks. "What's wrong with this place this morning? Did someone forget to pay the electric bill or something?"

"I don't know, but something doesn't seem right, does it?" Da Juan replies.

The boys keep walking, becoming more puzzled the closer they get to the dining room. Finally arriving, they find no one in the dining room, and only dim lights around the room. Looking at each other in disbelief, neither can figure out what is going on. "This makes no sense, Sterling. Joey said it's eight thirty, right?" Da Juan asks.

"Dude, we both looked at the alarm clock. Are we losing it?" Sterling replies.

"Okay, enough of this. Let's find a clock down here," Da Juan grumbles.

"I know; let's go to the front desk," Sterling says, sure he has the right answer.

"Good idea, let's go."

Down the hall and around the next corner the boys sprint to the front desk, alarming the receptionist. Seeing the startled look on her face, Sterling apologizes. "Oh, we're sorry, but could you tell us what time it is, please?"

"Of course. It's five forty-five," she says, pointing to the large clock across the room.

Shocked, both boys' mouths fell wide open. They look at each other for a moment, stunned. "Is everything all right?" the receptionist asks.

"Umm, did any of our group come down already?" Da Juan asks.

"No, you two are the first I have seen today. Are you sure they're awake already?"

"At this point, I'm not sure about anything," Sterling says. "But thank you."

The boys head back toward the elevator, shaking their heads in disbelief. "I just don't get it, Sterling," Da Juan says, wearied from it all.

"I know. Did we both really just dream all of that? Is that even possible?" Sterling asks, frustrated.

Back up the elevator, back around the corner and down the quiet hallway they go. Sterling slides the room key through the scanner and the lock clicks, allowing him to open the door. They step into the room, still dimly lit by the solitary lamp on the nightstand. Sterling tosses the key onto the table, while Da Juan shuts and locks the door. "What do ya say we get a couple of hours of sleep, then get up and head downstairs before everyone else, and nobody has to know about this?" Da Juan says.

"You got it," Sterling says, as he clicks the light switch.

Just as the two settle back down into their beds and relax, the lights come on and screams fill the room. Terrified, the boys jump in their beds. Da Juan rolls off onto the floor, and Sterling starts swatting at the air.

"Aah, we got you!" the rest of the teens all scream out, then begin to laugh.

The boys come to a stop and as their eyes adjust to the light again, they realize all of their friends have just pranked them. "Oh, my goodness, you guys scared us to death," Sterling says, gasping for breath.

Da Juan, tired and sluggish and trying to comprehend the whirlwind of activity before his eyes, raises himself off the floor onto his knees, leaning on the bed. He looks over to Sterling, who is looking back at him. The whole group pauses for a moment, awaiting Da Juan's response. He takes a deep breath and shakes his head, "Whew!" he says. "That was awesome."

At that, everyone piles in on the two bewildered teens.

Chapter Seventeen

We are here to help

That was crazy, wasn't it? Totally, from way out in left field. I wish you could've seen the faces on those two. They are not used to being the ones on the receiving end of a prank from us. It was great! The best thing was, it wasn't even planned. It had been storming that night, for a couple of hours. Really hard stuff, too: a lot of thunder and lightning. When Sterling and Da Juan were awakened, Raul heard them and came up with the plan, since he and Joey had an adjoining room with them. Once they dozed back off, Raul and Joey tiptoed in and changed the alarm clock and took their cell phones, turning on the flashlight mode and placing them behind the curtains so the glow would seem like the morning sun. Pretty devious, huh? Well, look at who we learned from. The rest was easy, since the hotel staff was more than happy to play along. Of course, after we all had a good laugh, we went back and got a couple of hours more sleep. Then we went down for breakfast like nothing had ever happened. If Mr. Fisher or Jason and Renee ever knew about it, they never said a word to us.

•••••••

As breakfast is winding down, chatter begins among the group as to what their open day should be filled with. Having already enjoyed all of their planned activities, they had allowed a couple of days at the end of the week to just wing it. There is a relaxing atmosphere throughout the dining room that is broken with the ringing of Mr. Fisher's cell phone.

"Hello?" Mr. Fisher answers, not recognizing the number showing on his phone. "Yes, this is he."

At first, no one else is really paying attention to his call. After a few moments, the others begin to be curious.

"I see. Yes. Well, we don't really have any plans for the next couple of days, so I guess we could possibly–." Tim says, but is interrupted.

The others all stop what they are doing and listen intently to find out what this conversation could be about that would have anything to do with the next couple of days.

"So, what happened to their store?" Tim says into the phone. He motions with one finger for everyone to wait just a moment longer. "And you say they did not have flood insurance?"

The group is sitting closer to the edge of their seats the longer this conversation continues.

"All right. Yes, it certainly seems like a wonderful opportunity for us. Give me just a moment to talk this over with the group. I will call you back shortly. Okay. Goodbye." Tim pulls the phone away from his ear and pushes the button to disconnect the call. Setting the phone down on the table, he looks up at all the impatient eyes looking back at him. "Okay, here's the deal," he says, speaking a bit louder to make sure everyone hears. "That was one of the pastors who had replied to us that he had no projects going on that would need our help." He pauses, taking a breath. "However, the storm that passed through here last night did a bit of damage before it got to us. There is a small independently-owned Christian book store about two hours away from us this morning that has suffered quite a bit of water damage due to some unexpected flash flooding from the storm. Would you guys be interested in helping the owners get the store back up and running? Oh yeah, they are asking because the owners did not have flood insurance."

Mr. Fisher looks around the room at the whole team. Everyone seems to have an agreeable look on their face, but he wants to make sure they all really do agree. "You guys talk this over, OK? I just want to make sure you understand that you don't have to, and if you do help out, it will mean giving up the remainder of the week's activities."

The group looks around at each other and they all nod their heads to Da Juan, who speaks up for everyone. "Mr. Fisher, helping is what we have in mind to do. I mean, don't get me wrong, we've all enjoyed the fun we've been having this week, but we're ready to go."

Smiling proudly, and looking a little bit corny, Mr. Fisher replies, "Well, OK then. I will call Pastor Williams back and let him know that we'll be there this afternoon."

•••••••

Next Summer

As the bus doors open and Tim steps off, right away he sees the imposing figure of a man heading directly for him. This man looks as though he would have no trouble breaking any or all of the group that has come into small pieces. His steps are bold and filled with purpose; for a split second, Tim ponders the thought that they are at the wrong place. Then a large smile stretches across the man's face, a smile almost as large as the man himself. Seeing this, Tim feels at ease and begins walking towards the man. Just as they are drawing close, they both extend right hands. The man takes Tim's hand and firmly but not overbearingly shakes it. "You must be Brother Tim," the deep voice says.

"I am," Tim confirms. "And you are?" he asks, hesitant to assume that this is the pastor.

"Oh, forgive me," the man says. "I am Pastor Williams. I spoke with you earlier."

"Yes, I was just a bit hesitant to assume."

"Of course. How was the trip?" Pastor Williams asks, as the group begins to roll out from the bus.

"It was fine."

"So, this is your group. It is so exciting to see young people get involved in service to the Lord," Pastor Williams says, waving to everyone as they step out. "Thank you so much for coming on such short notice, and welcome. I know you have a schedule to keep, so if it's OK, I'd like to show you around."

Everyone follows the pastor into the store. Obvious signs of water damage are all around. Mud is all over the sidewalk and in the carpet, going several inches up the wall. The bottoms of all the shelves are in disarray, and many things are strewn throughout the store. "Wow," can be heard throughout the group as they look at the damage.

"Things could have been much worse, and if the sisters had flood insurance we wouldn't be standing here right now. Although they thought they were covered, their insurance agent is telling them their policy did not include flood damage."

"So, what do we do? How can we help?" Jason asks. Everyone is walking about, taking it all in.

"Well, I would like to treat this sort of like those home shows I see on TV," Pastor Williams says. "You know, kick them out and fix the place, and then bring them back and surprise them".

"Oh, I get it. So, where are the sisters?" Tim joins in with a gleam in his eye.

"They were here this morning, and called me when they opened the door and found the mess. Once I had spoken with you, brother Tim, I sent them away for the day to get in touch with their suppliers, to get new materials in quickly. I told them I had a crew coming, and that we would take care of things. They will be back tomorrow morning."

"So, I'm guessing demo is the word of the day today?" Tim asks.

"Did I hear the word demo?" Sterling asks.

"Grr! Grr, grr," sounds out amongst all of the boys, as they all do their best Tim Allen impersonations.

"I knew that would be coming next," Kendra says, shaking her head.

"Demo is wicked awesome fun, Kendra," Joey says. Enthusiastically, he bear hugs Kendra, lifting her up off the floor.

"It's not going to be 'wicked awesome fun' for you if you don't put me down, you lunatic," she fires back at him. He quickly complies.

"You guys have so much energy," Pastor Williams says, passing out tools. "I think it's just great."

"Speaking of demo, Pastor Williams, you look like you could just smack those big arms and hands of yours around and take care of everything," Da Juan says, squeezing the pastor's biceps.

"Well, I was a bodybuilder in my younger days. Never could make to the pros, though," he replies. "And I do try to stay in shape. So, you guys ready? Let's get on our PPE and get at it."

"PPE? What?" Sterling chimes in.

Quickly informing him, Allison retorts, "You know, personal protective equipment?" She pauses and looks at him. "Oh, just put on your safety glasses and gloves."

•••••••

Two and a half days later, the team brings the sisters back in to see their newly-renovated bookstore. As they come to the front door, they can see right away that the sign has been repainted. "Oh, Connie, look at the sign," Carol says, holding her sister's arm.

"I know! And look at the planter boxes, with those beautiful flowers," Connie adds.

Pastor Williams holds the door handle, waiting for the sisters to come closer. "Well, sisters, can I assume you like what you see so far?"

They move closer to the door, examining everything outside and enjoying the fresh new look. "Now Pastor, you know very well that we do; it just looks so inviting out here," Carol replies as they make it to the door and walk in.

"Oh, my word," Connie says, a tear slowly falling down her cheek.

Pastor Williams follows them through the door, resting his hands on their shoulders as they look about the store in awe. Their hearts are overwhelmed at the sight of new laminate flooring and freshly painted walls, all in soft relaxing shades. In one corner sits a coffee table and two chairs for customers to sample read. Against another wall, there is a soft rug for children to sit on and look through picture books. All of the old wooden shelves have been replaced with brand new units that look as shiny as the new books they hold. Together, they hold their hands in the air and look up to the heavens as they softly say, "Thank you, Lord."

"That's right, sisters, God is good, isn't he?" Pastor Williams whispers to them.

"All the time," Connie replies.

"And all the time," Carol adds.

"God is good," they all finish.

"Well sisters, I want you to meet the team that came in and helped me pull this off in such a short time," Pastor Williams says. He motions to the door, and the whole group begins filing in. "These folks are this year's graduating class from Pinnacle Christian School. They came out here this week and worked hard to help me, and they are the reason your store looks so wonderful."

The group files in, everyone clapping their hands and smiling. Once they are all inside, Mr. Fisher raises his hand to speak. "Ladies, we have heard from your pastor of the way you two have been such a help to folks over the years, and how this store has been in your family for so long. It has truly been our pleasure to help you this week. Thank you for all you do, and as the old timers used to say, 'keep on keepin' on.'"

Chapter Eighteen

A little of this and a little of that

Miss Connie and Miss Carol were so nice. They wanted to be a part of the renovations, but their pastor talked them into hanging out with Renee and Jason for a couple of days. After the demo on the first day, we had all of their stock inventoried and separated, good from bad. Renee and Jason helped them to find new things for the store, and then took them on a couple of fun day trips. Renee said they were so fun to be around. She said they talked a lot about the days when they were kids, and how the town was back then. There seemed to be nothing about their town history that Miss Connie and Miss Carol didn't know. I don't think there was a dry eye in the store as we watched Connie and Carol looking over everything. When they cried, we cried. It was a really special time.

Of course, it wasn't all crying. We got to see what Da Juan looks like with drywall dust all in his 'fro. And our macho guys were definitely a riot to watch, especially compared to Pastor Williams; that man is a mountain. There were late nights and long days, but it was great. It was over before we realized it. Then we loaded up and headed down the road to begin our schedule. Our first stop was to help out at a food pantry and soup kitchen ministry. This one was the easiest one to choose and schedule, since Jason was already working with them every year to raise money and collect food to help keep them going. Easy peasy, right?

•••••••

"Jason, Renee, it's so good to see you, again. How have you been?" Shelly asks, hugging them both.

"We've been well," Renee says, as she is pulling out of the embrace.

"It's so good to finally be back," Jason adds.

"We are so glad you're here. So, how is the happy couple?"

Renee and Jason look at each other and then back at Shelly. "Well..." Jason starts, hesitantly.

"What? Come on now, no holding out on me. What's going on?" Shelly playfully scolds.

"I'm pregnant," Renee bursts out, smiling from ear to ear.

"Are you serious? Don't mess with me."

"Yeah, very serious."

"Ooh! Congratulations!" Shelly squeals, grabbing both of them into a bear hug and shaking them relentlessly. "You must have just found out," she continues, pulling away and looking back and forth between the two.

"Well, *I* just found out. In fact, I just found out in front of a whole stadium full of baseball fans," Jason playfully smirks.

"You didn't!" Shelly says, grinning at Renee.

Smiling and nodding, Renee confesses.

"You little bugger, you. Good job. I love it," Shelly says, grinning and winking at Renee. Leaning over towards Jason, she whispers, "That just means it's your turn to surprise *her* now."

"Well, I'm not about to get pregnant, if that's what you're thinking," he says facetiously.

"Oh, why not?" Renee chimes in. "We can do it together."

"You guys are too much." Shelly shakes her head and smiles. "So, I see your team is raring to go," she says, motioning to the group behind them. "How 'bout we take a quick tour and show everyone what we do?"

"Yeah, let's go!" the whole group yells out their answer

Startled, Shelly jumps and looks back at everyone. "Oh, OK; it's gonna be like that, huh?"

•••••••

The team has settled into their duties for the day. Some are organizing dry goods as they are unloaded from the trucks. Others deliver them to their locations in the warehouse. Still others pull the supplies from those locations to fill orders for the items, to be delivered to locations around the city that will use the food for soup kitchens and pantries for those in need. Being a large food ministry for both US shelters and overseas ministries, there is always much to do.

"How do you keep up with all of this stuff?" Allison asks Shelly.

"It's definitely a lot of planning and careful watching of things," she replies. "The amazing thing is that we are not a full-time facility, per se. We do have a handful of paid employees who tend to things on a daily basis. However, the rest of all you see going on in here is done by volunteers. We have folks who can only help out every now and again, and folks who are pretty regular. People help as God lays it on their heart to do."

"So, all of the organizing and planning is done by paid employees?"

"That's right," Shelly responds. "And we have one person who coordinates all of the volunteers."

Just then, Sterling drives by on a vehicle resembling a golf cart pulling a wagon, carrying a full payload of boxes and bags of items heading to the shipping dock, where they will be loaded into a van and delivered to a nearby soup kitchen. "Look at me, Allison, no hands!" he crows, his hands in the air and a huge, crazy smile on face. As he is passing them, he turns his body to continue smiling at them but his elbow hits the steering wheel, causing the cart to swerve and throwing a few boxes onto the floor. "Oh, no! My fault," he says, slamming on the brakes, bringing the vehicle to a squealing stop. "I'll clean it up," he says, jumping off and getting to work loading his fallen cargo back onto the wagon.

Allison shakes her head at Sterling and turns back to Shelly. "Oddly, I was just thinking how surprised I was that he hadn't done anything like that yet." Shelly smiles back at Allison and then turns back to watch as Sterling picks up the casualties. "Do you think I jinxed him?"

"Maybe, but I kinda doubt it." Shelly turns back to Allison. "You know, it's that type of thought process that made me think that you would be perfect to work with Karen, coordinating the work."

Puzzled, Allison asks Shelly, "Really? How so?"

"You know your friends very well, and I'll bet you pick up on others' characteristics very quickly also. Let's go."

Chapter Nineteen

Now that's what I call a buffet line

Me coordinating the work... I gotta say, I didn't see that coming. It's very scary and intimidating to step into a role that pops up out of nowhere. Granted, this was only for a few days—but in some ways, I felt like I was being groomed for something. I mean, where did the thought of me being in a leadership role even come from? Am I just being paranoid? My mind kept going back to what Renee had said, about us not being able to fool her. Was she influencing these people to put us in these roles to see how we would react? To see if we were up to the task at hand? Would she do that? If she did, would it be a bad thing—or is she really such a good personality reader that she is just trying to push us in the direction that she thinks we're sure to go eventually? Am I nuts? Am I blowing this whole thing out of proportion? I mean, I did enjoy the week. Not to say I like the thought of being in charge, because I really don't. I have always seen myself as being just another worker bee, plugging along, getting the job done. However, watching Karen work her magic was enlightening. She actually had her hands in *everything*. I mean, I always thought of that kind of position as being a puppet master: you know, pulling strings and making people move. Karen isn't like that at all. Yes, she puts people in the right place to get the job done, but then she moves throughout the whole operation, jumping in and helping out if needed and then moving on. She is like a machine! Could I be like that, a multi-tasker on steroids? IDK; it has definitely given me plenty to think about. But I digress; I guess I do that a lot, huh?

OK, so, getting back to our journey. After spending a week in the warehouse stocking shelves and processing orders to send food and other needed items to local and not-so-local pantries, and other places where people in need can be helped, we went to local soup kitchens and homeless shelters to actually help individuals. This was ministering at its very core. It turns out that in the city and outlying areas, there are a number of shelters where food and/or a place to sleep are offered, as well as a god message.

While Jason and Mr. Fisher were preaching and speaking with people one on one about the Lord, the rest of us were cooking, cleaning, and serving tables and plates in buffet lines.

•••••••

"Dude, that net is not gonna cover your 'fro," Sterling says, shaking his head.

Da Juan is pulling and tugging and trying to stuff his rather large head of hair into the average-to-small hair net that was handed to him. Kendra comes over and lends a hand in the struggle. Sterling smiles and chuckles, and videos the failing project with his phone.

"Bro, you're not helping things here," Da Juan protests.

"Sorry, my 'Mad Fro Bro,' I'll put it away," Sterling apologizes, and puts his cell phone in his pocket. "All right, what can I do to help?"

"Just hold this side. I think we almost have it," Kendra quickly answers.

As Sterling reaches for his side of the hairnet, the pressure from the mountain of hair can be contained no longer and the net flies off Da Juan's head. It lands on Miss Della's shoulder as she stirs a pot of her homemade tomato soup. Raising an eyebrow and turning to the three teens who have frozen in their tracks, she looks down at the small projectile. She taps her spoon on the side of the pot and lays it down on the counter beside the stove top. Walking over to the group, Miss Della takes off her chef's hat and wiggles it onto Da Juan's head, then picks the hair net off of her shoulder and pulls it into place on her own head. "What do you say you help me today, Mr. Da Juan?" she says, motioning to him with her index finger as she turns to walk back to her pot.

"Yes, Ma'am," Da Juan replies meekly, and follows her like a scolded puppy.

Sterling and Kendra stand there for just a second, speechless, then burst into laughter as he walks off.

•••••••

As the day comes to a close, everyone is worn out from all of the excitement of trying to keep up with the seemingly endless line of those in need. The youngsters are exhausted, but there is still work to be done. There is a teen sitting somewhere, in any direction you look. Miss Della says goodbye to the last guest and shuts the door. Making her way back into the kitchen, she spots the teens almost asleep. "What do you kids think you're doing?" she says, standing with her hands on her hips.

"We're just so *tired*," Sterling whines.

"Yeah, that was brutal," Da Juan adds.

"Brutal?" Miss Della scoffs. "This was an easy day for me, because I had all of you here with me. Imagine doing this with less help."

Everyone's jaws fell open. "We didn't even think it about like that."

"It's all right my dears," Miss Della continues. "I'm very glad to have had the help. I don't do this alone. I just don't usually have this many people, so, you did very much help out today."

Everyone began responding, telling her that they were glad to have been here today, and that they were happy they could help. Just as they all began to relax and rest a moment in their accomplishments, Miss Della speaks up again.

"Yes, it has been wonderful. But we're not done yet, so get yourselves up before I take a switch to the lot of you," she says, with the sweetest grandma look on her face that has ever been seen.

"But what about—" Sterling begins, but is cut off.

"Dear, we have to finish cleaning up, and prepare for next week," Miss Della interrupts.

A collective moan of agony waves over the room, and they all stand up.

Chapter Twenty

Taking it to the streets: preaching, that is

I honestly don't know how Miss Della does it. She provides meals for an endless sea of people in need. Well, I suppose it really wasn't endless, but when you are serving plates and just they keep coming, it sure feels endless. When she said that she didn't do it alone, we wondered where her team was that day, while we were there. It turns out that a lot of the people helping her are some of the folks she is feeding. They actually come in and help her cook and set up the meal. Of course, it is only a few that do so, but they do help her. They love her for what she does. Imagine, an eighty-five-year-old woman who has been feeding the homeless for twenty years, ever since she retired. Different churches in the area will come from time to time and give a message for the guests as they dine. Some don't like that; I could tell as Jason and Mr. Fisher were preaching that many were annoyed, but many enjoyed it as well. No one left before they had finished eating. Miss Della is so warm and loving; throughout the time folks are eating, she finds time to walk around and check on them, giving out hugs to everyone. It was hard work. We washed tables and dishes, delivered plates and bottles of water, and cooked the food. We also had a wonderful time. It is hard to see so many people struggling. I can definitely understand why Miss Della would want to help them. I just don't understand how she does it every day, every week. She has such a love for people and a huge heart that cannot turn anyone away. She is amazing, but she is the first to tell you that it is the Lord that keeps her going. We enjoyed our time with Miss Della, and then we stepped out if her frying pan and into the fire.

Next Summer

••••••

The church bus comes to a stop in front of Emmanuel Baptist Mission on seventh street. One by one, the group steps down onto the hot summer pavement. "Wow," Da Juan says, wiping his brow right away. "I thought Miss Della's kitchen was hot last week, but this is something else."

"I know. This is unbearable," Sterling agrees.

"I'm sure the church has air conditioning, guys," Allison says, half trying to put their minds at ease and half trying to stop the complaints before they spread.

Each person steps off the bus and lets out an oppressed sigh as the heat hits them in the face. A moment later, they sigh in relief as they step through the church doors and into the cool, sweet, conditioned air. The auditorium is quiet as they file through in a single line behind Mr. Fisher. Just as the group reaches the pulpit, a woman comes through the door on the left side.

"Tim Fisher?" the lady says in a quiet voice, extending her hand with a smile.

Tim reaches for her hand and shakes it. "Yes Ma'am. How are you today?"

"I am fine, and I hope you and your fine-looking group are fine, as well," she replies, smiling at the group. Receiving many smiles and nods, she continues. "As you probably have guessed, I am Sister Walker, the church secretary. I spoke with you a while back."

"Yes, yes," Tim replies. "We are looking forward to meeting your pastor and being a help this week."

"Yes, and while we wait for him we want to thank you for such strong air conditioning. It feels so good in here," Da Juan says in his most diplomatic tone.

A chorus of resounding agreement follows him from all of the rest of the group.

"Well, let me say on behalf of the church, thank you, and I am very sorry," Sister Walker says, also trying to sound diplomatic.

"Sorry? Sorry for what?" Jason asks.

"Pastor Henry didn't inform you of how you will be helping him this week, did he?"

Tim, now visibly puzzled and just a bit apprehensive, replies. "Uh, no, he didn't. All he said to me was that he had a very important project, and that he felt that the Lord sent us to be a vital part in its completion."

Nodding and smiling, Sister Walker continues, "That's my pastor. Well, he left me word to ask you and your team to join him at the intersection of Third and Calvin Streets. He asked that you all walk down, as it is only about three blocks from here."

"Really? That's odd," Renee comments.

"No, not really. Not for Pastor Henry," Sister Walker explains. "Just turn right once you're outside and walk three blocks, then turn left and walk two more."

"Thank you, Sister, and we will see you in a while," Jason says.

"How will we recognize him, Sister? Mr. Fisher asks.

"Oh, trust me; you'll recognize him."

"Um, well, OK then," Tim says, then turns to the group. "Let's go guys."

"We're not seriously gonna walk five blocks in this sweltering heat, are we?" Kendra asks, afraid of the answer.

"It's not really the heat, it's the humidity," Joey says.

"Um, no, I think it's both," Allison corrects, a bit sarcastically.

"OK, OK, let's get going. We came to help. If Pastor Henry wants us to walk, there must be a reason," Renee says, motioning for everyone to move along.

Sister Walker watches in pity as the group files out the door, into the heat and humidity.

•••••••

Four blocks and twenty minutes later, the group comes within earshot of a loud booming voice that sounds like it's about a block away. Looking straight ahead, soon they all see a man standing near the corner with a Bible in one hand, the other motioning to passersby. Scripture flows from his lips as if it has always been there, never being extinguished. "Is that Pastor Henry?" Sterling asks, leaning in close to Da Juan.

"I would say so, Sterling," Renee answers.

As Pastor Henry spots the group, now only a few feet away, he begins to walk towards them. "Good morning, how are you on God's great day?"

"We are fine, Pastor Henry. How are you?" Tim responds.

"I also am well," he replies, then looks at the group. "Good morning, group."

Everyone begins to respond in kind. "Well, Pastor, how can we be of help to you? I'm afraid none of us have any street preaching experience," Tim says.

"That's OK," Pastor Henry replies. "Around the next block, there is a small park. Let us go there to talk for a few moments, so that we do not block the sidewalk." Waving them on to follow him, Pastor Henry begins the journey, pulling a small dolly behind him that holds a single cardboard box. The group follows Pastor Henry to the park, and everyone finds a place to sit. Pastor Henry tells them, "I am a street preacher. God has called me to that, but I want you to know that I have prayed for God to send me help in spreading the news about my work here. This is a big city, with many people. People I want to reach out to. So, as I said, I have been praying for help; then I received your email, offering help. So, God has answered my prayers."

"Well, we are definitely here to help. So, what is it that we can do?" Jason asks.

"In this box are flyers about our church," he says. Motioning to the box by his side, he picks it up. Reaching inside, he pulls out a handful of flyers and hands them to Tim, Renee, and Jason.

Looking the flyer over, front to back, Tim says, "Hand out flyers? That's all you want us do?"

"It is more than a simple act, Brother," Pastor Henry replies.

"You know, the people I've seen this morning all look like they're in a really big hurry. Will they even take a flyer from us? How do we do it?" Allison asks.

"Well, some will take them, and some will not. Don't let that bother you. It's hard for some to stand out and do this sort of thing. Just be polite and offer it. If they won't take it, it's OK." The pastor explains, "I want to cover as much of this city as possible." Pulling out a map of the city, Pastor Henry describes his plan. "I want us to break up into pairs and stand at different intersections. Then every couple of hours, we will move to another block. Following this plan, we can canvas the city in a week's time. Or at least most of it," he says, smiling. "You will help me reach so many more people than I would be able to reach alone."

"Then let's get going," Raul speaks up.

"Very good, young man. Why don't you hang with me today?" Pastor Henry replies.

"Cool beans, let's go."

Moments later, everyone has been given their street corner assignments, and the pairs are coming up to get handfuls of flyers. Da Juan and Sterling bounce to the front to get their supply, clearly excited. "Awesome. Handing out flyers," Sterling says, and the two run down the street, immediately handing out flyers to everyone they pass.

Shaking her head, Allison, watches the two overly exuberant teens fly down the street. "Of course. They're even good at this."

Chapter Twenty-One

Take up your cross and follow me

I know, know, I really need to get over this, right? Trust me, I love those guys. I am just so amazed by how they seem to be able to just pick up anything and run with it— and yes, I'm a bit envious, even though I know I shouldn't be. Granted, I'm only eighteen, but I have never seen anything like it. They're like two golden boys. I mean, who has two golden boys in one group? One, yeah, OK. But *two*? That's unheard of, right? And yes, I am working on my envy problem. A lot of prayer is involved here. But hey, admitting you have a problem is the first and hardest step. Am I right, or am I right? You know, it's not that I want them to fail, or anything like that. I just want to be better at things, like they are, I suppose.

Once again, I digress. Pastor Henry is awesome, just so ya know. I've never seen a street preacher before, so that was a very different experience for me. For all of us, I think. We all had a chance to spend time with him so we could see him at work. I don't think I have enough nerve to do that. I was nervous just standing there with him and handing out flyers. It's kinda like those people in New York City who walk the street and hand out flyers for comedy clubs and whatnot. Some people will take it from you and give it a once-over, or maybe even stick it in their pocket. Some people will take and hold it until they walk past a trash can, and drop it in. Other people will politely decline and walk away, and still others will cross the street to avoid you. Then, there are those people who are absolutely outraged that you would dare want to talk to them about God. They will tell you that you have no right to impose your beliefs on them. We only encountered a few of those, thankfully. One guy actually tried to get a policeman to arrest Pastor Henry for disturbing the peace. How he kept his cool through that one, I will never know. Pastor Henry just kept this serene look on his face and talked quietly with the officer and the irate man. It really was something to see. Incidentally, I think you know me well enough by now to know that would not fly with me. To be fair, there were also people who thanked us for inviting them and others to church. We also had several folks who stopped and prayed with us. Of course, the dramatic tends to come to mind first, but it was a great experience and Pastor Henry said we did him a tremendous favor (his actual words). So, there you go.

From there we went to help a fledgling ministry. One of the pastors we heard back from asked us to come and help his youth group. They were just getting started with a puppet ministry, and he hoped that since he had seen some photographs of puppet skits on our church website, we might have some pointers for them. We all decided to do better than that. There is a Christian puppet company that holds conferences all over the country. Mr. Fisher, having formerly been part of our church's puppet group, knew that there would be a conference somewhere in the area. He looked it up and had us schedule our week there for that time. It was wonderful to surprise those guys with a trip to the conference. There were so many things for them to see and do, including classes that everyone could sign up for to learn techniques. We were also able to surprise them with a shopping spree. Those guys were like kids in a candy store. They picked out some lights, some new puppets, and some learning DVDs. We all enjoyed competing in the different performance categories, but of course none of us won. The conference went on for three days, all afternoons, so we helped them with prop building for their first original play. One of their team members had written a skit based on *The Godfather*, that mafia movie. He called his play *God the Father,* and the main character was an ex-mob guy turned preacher. They performed the skit for us all on our last night there with them. It was a real treat for us to see some of the work that we had put in being celebrated. They did a wonderful job. I believe their team is gonna be a blessing to a lot of kids—and adults, too.

The next morning, we set out on the road again. Our plan was to surprise the next church by coming a day early, since we had finished early with the puppet work. However, when we stopped for lunch, we saw something that changed our minds.

••••••

Holding her drink with her straw in her mouth, but not actually drinking, Kendra stares out the restaurant window.

"Earth to Kendra. Earth to Kendra; come in, Kendra," Raul says facetiously, waving his hands in front of her face.

Shaking her head and trying to focus on him, she replies, "Huh? What?"

"You OK?" Allison asks, then chuckles.

"Yeah, yeah, I'm fine..." she replies, distractedly.

Raul and Allison turn to look out the window to see what Kendra is so interested in. "What are you looking at?" they both ask.

Pointing out the window of the restaurant, Kendra draws their attention to a figure moving slowly near the highway, across the shopping center lot. "I'm just trying to figure out what that is moving near the road. Do you see it?"

Looking with his eyes squinted, as if that increases the distance he is able to see, Raul says. "I don't see anything; where is it?"

"I think I see it," Allison says. "Are you pointing all the way over to the traffic on the highway?"

"Yes! What is it?" Kendra says, walking over to the window.

Allison and Raul join her. All three stand in front of the window like marble statues facing the highway, about a thousand feet away.

Da Juan, noticing the scene, speaks up. "What's up guys? Have you been bad, so you have to stand with your noses to the glass?"

"Ha ha, very funny," Kendra replies sarcastically, turning to glare at him and then back to the window. "We're trying to figure out what that thing moving over by the road is."

One by one, the rest of the group stands to see the mysterious figure moving slowly amid the backdrop of moving traffic off in the distance. "It sorta looks like a cross," Joey says.

"Yeah, that's it," Raul agrees.

"Yeah, a man dragging a cross—and that thing is *huge*," chimes in Sterling.

Renee, hearing all of the commotion and watching the group's reactions, could sense something was coming from all of it. Leaning in close to Jason, she whispers, "How much longer before our plans for the day are changed?"

"Well, if I were a betting man," he whispers back, "I'd say that the plans have already been changed."

Just then, Kendra approaches the couple and Brother Tim. "We don't technically have to be at our next stop for a couple of days, right?" she asks, with a

Next Summer

curious look on her face.

Tim looks across the table at Renee and Jason, who give him a look that says, "Just let them do what they want." Looking back at Kendra, he smiles and says, "That's right. What do you have in mind?"

Behind them at the window, the others are watching and listening to see what she will ask.

"Well, I was thinking, the guy over there dragging the cross is going in the same direction as we need to go," Kendra says timidly.

"Yes," Tim agrees.

"And, we do have a little time to spare."

"Yes."

"So, I was thinking..."

"Yes..."

"Oh, for the love of Pete, just spit it out!" Allison barks, losing patience.

Kendra glances at Allison, startled, then turns back to Tim. "OK, OK! We should walk with him," she blurts out quickly, as if ripping off a Band-Aid.

"And there it is," Renee whispers to Jason, who only smiles his acknowledgement of the comment.

"I mean, if he will let us," Kendra adds.

"You mean, like just follow him while he drags that thing down the road?" Joey asks.

"I mean, if he doesn't mind, we could take short turns, too. It would give him a break," Da Juan adds.

"Yes, exactly. That's all I'm saying," Kendra explains. "You know, just to show support for what he is doing."

"Well, I'm all for supporting our brothers and sisters in Christ, but we need to speak with him first to see what he wants. After all, this is his ministry," Mr. Fisher agrees, with conditions. "And if he is willing to have the company, how far do you want to walk with him?"

Kendra turns to the group to put the question to them. They all huddle up close to discuss the matter. "OK guys, I know this was my idea, but what do you think?" Kendra asks hopefully.

They all look at each other for a moment, lifting eyebrows and shrugging shoulders.

"OK, look; this kind of stuff is why we came. When will we ever have this opportunity again? I say we walk all the way to the next church, or as far as we can. And I think we need to take turns carrying the cross," Kendra says.

The group looks around at one another, and everyone begins to nod in agreement. When the group turns back to their teacher, Kendra speaks. "We would all like to go with him for as long as the road and time will allow, and even take turns carrying the cross—if he will allow us to," she says, nodding to Mr. Fisher.

"I suppose, then, that we should travel ahead and wait for you?" Tim asks.

The group nods in unison, and Tim hears everyone say, "Yes."

"Well then, go ahead out there and meet with him to figure this out. We will wait here for one of you to call back and let us know," Renee says.

Kendra stands perfectly still for a moment, thinking, and blinks several times. Then she turns and funnels the group out the door and on their way. The three chaperones watch them as they walk out. As soon as the restaurant door closes, Jason and Tim both turn to Renee with a deer-in-the-headlights look on their faces.

Shifting her eyes back and forth between the two, Renee finally answers the question they both want to ask. "What? Are we going to do everything for them? This has been their trip all along, so if they want to make decisions, let them do the leg work."

The two men take another sip from their sodas and say nothing.

"Stop worrying, they'll be fine."

Chapter Twenty-Two

Ah, the smell of lake water and pine trees

I know. That kinda threw us all for a loop, especially Kendra. We never expected them to just say, "Go; do!" We didn't think they would just sit and wait while we walked with this man carrying his cross. In between the restaurant and making it out to where the gentleman was walking, we had talked it all out. The man was very nice. He seemed glad that anyone had stopped by to encourage him. He told us that he had been carrying that cross for several days by himself, and had plans to go on for some days to come. The cross was very heavy and most of us could not manage it by ourselves, so we doubled up. He told us the idea had come to him in the middle of the night. He'd dismissed it as a silly idea at first, but it just would not leave his mind. Pushing it away for several weeks did nothing to ease its pull on him, so finally he gave in and began to pray. He told us that once he did, the ideas of what and how flooded his mind, mostly at night while he slept.

The cross definitely was not made for comfort. About sixteen feet long, I'd say, give or take, made from a white pine tree, it had that crackly-looking bark that kinda dug into your arms and shoulders as you carried it. Yes, it still had the bark, and even some knots for good measure. Mr. White said he wanted it to be difficult to carry so it would remind him that when Christ carried his, it was no stroll in the park. Oh yeah, the man's name was John White; sorry, I should have said that earlier. We were soon all horribly sweaty, and had little bits of bark stuck to and down inside our clothes. I don't think any of us came away without scratches on our necks and arms, and most of us had little bruises, but it was one of the best things I've ever experienced. Mr. White is such a nice person and while he'd set out to make his journey alone, he thanked us over and over for sharing a portion of it with him.

....

As the bus pulls into the campground, all of the sweaty teens have finally cooled down from the air conditioning. There are people everywhere. Parents are dropping off their children. Vendors bring in supplies for the next two weeks. Last minute touches are put in place to welcome the summer campers, as well as the camp counselors. Da Juan heads up the group stepping down off of the bus and into the beautiful setting of a perfect summer day. "Man, this place is awesome," he says. Arms stretched wide, he takes in a deep breath with his eyes closed. "Bro, smell this place. The pine trees are intoxicating."

"I know," Sterling replies. "Reminds me of all of those summers out here."

"I know."

"Why did we ever stop coming?"

"You two were just here last summer, you boneheads," Allison chides. "Now move along."

"Yeah, we need to get to work signing in all these campers," Kendra adds, as the two girls walk past the daydreamers.

The rest of the group follows along, and Da Juan and Sterling run to catch up. "Can't we even take a shower first?" Sterling whines.

Renee answers, exasperated. "We've been over this. Getting here late like we did doesn't leave time for that."

"You could just go jump in the lake," a voice behind them says.

The whole group stops and turns around to see who this voice belongs to. When they turn, they see Mr. and Mrs. Taylor, the owners of the camp. "You could jump in the lake to cool down. If you like," he repeats.

"Hey, Mr. and Mrs. Taylor. How are you?" Da Juan and Sterling say, pulling them into a group hug.

"We're fine, boys. How are you two?" Mrs. Taylor says, smiling.

"We're good, too." Sterling says.

"Hey, do we have enough time for a quick jump in the lake? No lie?" Da Juan asks.

"Sure, just be back in ten minutes," Mr. Taylor kindly says, knowing they feel sweaty.

At that the whole group runs to the lake and onto the pier, diving one after the other into the warm lake.

Renee watches in amazement that the whole group ran off. "I knew Da

Next Summer

Juan and Sterling would go, but I really didn't expect them *all* to."

"That's good, though; that's what camp is about. When they come back, we'll get you guys set up," Mrs. Taylor adds.

•••••••

Walking toward the cabins, Sterling double counts the ten boys he has been assigned to chaperone, making sure none have run off and slipped out of his sight. All the campers have been checked in and are dropping off their belongings at a bunk that they will sleep on for the next two weeks. Sterling opens the door to the cabin that he and his ten boys will share, and everyone runs inside. He sees that one boy is a bit smaller than the others; he is left behind as they choose bunks. Keeping an eye out for him, Sterling gives some instructions to the group. "OK guys, get your things settled, and let's head down to the pavilion for the opening ceremony from Mr. Taylor."

One by one the boys finish placing their things how they want them and bolt out the door, running straight toward the pavilion. Matthew is still left behind as all the rest of the boys leave. "Matthew, are you doing OK?" Sterling asks.

"Almost done," Matthew timidly replies.

"Is this your first time at camp?" Sterling asks, walking closer to him.

"Yes."

"Well, it's great here, and you will have a wonderful time."

"OK," Matthew replies, apparently unconvinced. He finishes placing his things and hurries around the side of his bunk, knocking his bag onto the floor in the process. "Oh, man," he says as things tumble out and slide across the floor.

"That's all right. I'll help you." Sterling reaches down to lend the boy a hand gathering everything. "Wait a minute," Sterling says, picking an item up off the floor. "Is this what I think it is?" he asks.

"I'm sorry. Should I not have brought that?" Matthew asks timidly.

With an evil smile, Sterling replies, "Oh, I'm *very* glad you brought this."

Puzzled, Matthew asks, "You are? Why?"

Sterling sits down on the cot in front of Matthew to explain. "You see, Matthew, my best friend Da Juan and I have spent quite a few years pulling practical jokes on each other. Do you know what I... What am I talking about, of *course* you know what a practical joke is. You have this. We get each other all the time, but this has been coming for thirteen years now, and you are gonna help me. Okay?"

Sterling's evil smile now duplicated on Matthew's face, the boy replies, "Yeah, let's do it."

•••••••

As Sterling and Matthew walk up to the pavilion to find Da Juan, Sterling is unwrapping a piece of chewing gum. Da Juan, noticing what he has, suddenly begins to swallow and lick his lips. "Dude, where'd you get that gum?" he asks desperately.

Looking back, forth, and behind himself, Sterling answers, "Bro, I got this from little Matthew. Hang on; oh, there he is." Trying to look innocent, he calls the boy over. "Matthew, do you have any more gum?" he asks.

"Uh, I think so. Let me check," Matthew says, reaching into his pocket.

"My bud Da Juan would like a piece, if you don't mind," Sterling says, motioning to a smiling Da Juan.

"Oh yeah, sure. Here it is," Matthew says, pulling the package from his pocket and holding it out for Da Juan to pull a stick from it.

With a relieved smile on his face, Da Juan reaches for the gum, firmly grabbing the stick that is protruding. *Bzzzt* the fake gum package vibrates through Da Juan's hand and arm. "I-ee!" Da Juan squeaks out, and jerks his hand back. Jumping up and down and holding his hand, he looks at the little boy in disbelief. Sterling is now laughing uncontrollably and pointing at Da Juan. Matthew stands between them, fake gum still in his hand and a satisfied smile on his face. "He put you up to this didn't he?" Da Juan says, shaking his head and smiling.

"Of course I did, Bro. Doesn't that seem familiar to you?" Sterling replies, very proud of himself.

"Familiar? Should it?" Da Juan answers, puzzled.

"Think about it, Dude. The first day we met."

"Oh!" Da Juan remembers his joke buzzer. "Man! You're right, Dude. Good job, getting me back when I didn't expect it," Da Juan congratulates Sterling.

•••••••

Dusk falls at the campground, but things are nowhere near slowing down. This is the last night, and everyone wants to savor every moment. Games of hide and seek and tag break out everywhere. Near the pavilion, the chaperones prepare for dinner by lighting a huge campfire. There is singing and dancing and joke telling as the joy of the past two weeks continues. Every camper

Next Summer

and chaperone alike has had an experience they will likely never forget. The mornings began with breakfast and Bible class. Then sports and nature hikes took over, from mid-morning to early afternoons. The daily message came after lunch, and was followed by a time of prayer. Projects and talent shows every evening followed dinner, rounding out the days.

Hot dogs sizzle on skewers as happy campers hold them close to the fire. Amber shadows flicker across faces, revealing smiles that have grown as the last thirteen days have come and gone. The group of graduates walk around the fire, making sure all the children are safe and that no one is burned. "Remember, we have a surprise dessert once everyone is finished with their hotdogs and beans," Da Juan proclaims.

"I bet I know what it is," the now talkative Matthew exclaims.

"What?" Sterling asks, hoping he is right.

"S'mores!" Matthew and his new friend Chris cry out, positive they are right.

"Yep, that's it," Allison confirms, bringing a box full of chocolate bars and marshmallows and setting it down on a log, far enough away that the fire won't melt them.

"I've been looking forward to this ever since I heard about it," Kendra says.

"Why? Are S'mores your favorite or something?" Allison asks.

"I don't know. I've never had one," Kendra admits.

Sterling happens by at that exact moment, and stops in his tracks. "*What?!*" he yells. "You've never had a S'more? You're killin' me, Smalls!"

"What? Who's Smalls? What are you talking about?" Allison jumps in.

"You know, *Smalls*," he replies, shrugging with his hands out. "*Sandlot?*"

Kendra raises her eyebrows and shakes her head.

"You know, *Sandlot!* The movie?" She looks at him with a blank stare. "It's only one of the greatest movies of all time." Still no response, from either Allison or Kendra. "Now you really *are* killing me," he says, shaking his head at the two girls. "Never mind."

"Can I show Kendra how to make a S'more, Sterling?" Matthew asks, jubilantly.

Patting him on the back, Sterling replies, "Yes, please. We need to help this girl out."

Chapter Twenty-Three

A life well lived

Sandlot. Honestly, those boys... It's like everything in life has to do with sports. No, Kendra and I had not seen it before that night, but we have since had a girls' night and watched it. I'm sorry, but I don't think there's any way that pretty lifeguard married that little squinty perv and had all those kids. I know, I know; it's just make believe anyway, but that author had to be way off. The guys always cheer for him all the way through the picture, but I just don't see it. I imagine you are probably weary of my rantings and ravings, though, so I will move on.

Camp turned out to be so much fun. I think we had just as good a time as the kids. It's nice to see them getting to know each other, Making new friends, learning and growing. There were a few who surrendered their hearts to Christ and were saved, which is always great to see. Oh my, I almost forgot! We all had the surprise of the summer during the last night's activities. We were told there would be a special singing duet. That was all we knew. Everyone talked about it for days, but no one knew who would be singing. Then the music started for the song "Jesus Friend of Sinners," and all of a sudden, our very own Jacob and Emily walked up on the stage with microphones in their hands. They laid down the most powerful rendition of that song that you would ever want to hear. We all just stood there with our jaws wide open in disbelief. It seems they had been practicing for some time, waiting for the right moment to spring it on us. When they were done, the whole place shook with cheering and applause. I never would have expected that from those two; they are always so quiet. It turns out they had been wanting to sing for some time, but were nervous. They saw the camp as a way to come out of hiding without the large crowd that we have at church. You should have seen the smiles on their faces when everyone cheered for them.

Next Summer

So, to recap, camp was a success. All of the kids had a great time. They learned a lot about the Lord, and there were no fatalities. Just kidding, but it really did go very well. When we left the camp, our next church did not have one big project, but rather many little ones. To that end, we were all split up. Cutting grass, mending fences, taking some folks shopping who couldn't get out by themselves. It was basically helping the deacons and deaconesses. Da Juan and myself had a particularly eye-opening time.

•••••••

"I want to thank you young people, and you 'a little bit older' people," Pastor Billings starts, smiling at the latter part of his comment as he looks towards Renee, Jason and Tim. "Thank you for coming out to be with us this week. As we told you, we don't have one large project, but rather many small projects that are large at heart. So, to that end, we are going to split everyone up and spread our reach all over town this week."

Pastor Billings begins to call out names, assigning them to a member of his church, and together they head out for their mission for the day. Coming to the end of the list, there were only Allison and Da Juan remaining. Looking at each other and then around the room, they notice that no one is left for them to go out with. Da Juan shrugs as if to say, "I don't know," when Allison seems to look to him for answers. Just then, Pastor Billings speaks again. "All right, Allison and Da Juan, I saved the two of you for last, because you will be accompanying my wife and I."

"Oh, OK," the two say at the same time, glancing at each other.

"Let's go back to my office while we wait for my wife, and I'll fill you in on what we will be doing," Pastor Billings says. He turns, walking down the hallway towards his office with the young pair following on his heels. "Have a seat," he offers, pointing towards a sofa against one of the side walls. He continues on around the side of his desk and sits as well. "My wife will be here soon," he informs them, relaxing in his desk chair. "She is going with us to the home of one of our long-time church members. The reason for our visit today is one of encouragement, and hopefully we can provide a little comfort as well. This couple is in their seventies and have been retired for a few years, but just as they were hoping to settle into a time of freedom from the grind of everyday work, life took a turn for the worse. They spent their lives doing the right things. Married for over fifty years, they were saved at a young age and spent years in church. Then as soon as they are ready to spend their golden years together, he is diagnosed with dementia." Pastor Billings is visibly shaken by what he has just told the teens.

The two look at each other, then back at the pastor. "Are you all right?" Allison asks.

"I'm sorry. Yes, I'm all right," he replies. "It's difficult to see a friend's life taken from him." Da Juan and Allison sit silently, waiting for him to continue, as he wipes his eyes. "Annie and Lloyd Bishop were here when I arrived, a young preacher trying to do a good job and be accepted. They helped me tremendously, especially during the first few years," Pastor Billings says, trying to catch the teens up to speed before his wife arrives. "He doesn't recognize any of us anymore, not even Annie. His health is beginning to fail now, so along with the cognitive problems, Annie now has to be his nurse as well. She does have help come in a couple of times during the week, at least. So, we try to visit as often as we can, just to be a help to them both."

Just then, Mrs. Billings makes it to the pastor's office and announces that it is time to go. They all make their way to the Billings' car, and soon they pull out onto the highway.

••••••••

Mrs. Billings knocks on the front door softly and waits for a response. After a moment, Mrs. Bishop comes to the door and quietly opens it. Smiling, she hugs Mrs. Billings and invites everyone in. "Good morning! Welcome, you must be Allison, and you must be Da Juan," she says, hugging each one respectively. "Thank you so much for coming to see us. As you can imagine, we don't get out much lately." They both say, "You're welcome," as they step past her and into the room. Mrs. Bishop's eyes now fixed on Pastor Billings, she says, "Good morning, Pastor. How are you today?" She holds out her arms to hug him.

"I'm fine, Dear. How are you doing today?" he replies in kind, pulling her into a hug. "How's Lloyd today?"

"I'm fine. Lloyd is tired today, and agitated. It hasn't been a good day so far for him. I think he recognized me for a while yesterday. He didn't say much, but he did reach over and hold my hand." The Pastor nods at the news, and everyone makes their way into the living room to chat.

Pastor and Mrs. Billings persuade Mrs. Bishop to take a break for a while and allow the pastor and Da Juan to keep Mr. Bishop company. She escorts them all into the bedroom where Lloyd is lying propped up in the bed. "Lloyd? Dear, Pastor Billings is here for a visit, and he has his wife and a couple of young people with him." She speaks to Lloyd softly, so as not to startle him. "Pastor Billings and his young friend are going to sit with you while I step out for a little while."

"It's nice to have visitors," he says, looking away from the television program he is watching to see his guests. "I hope you haven't come far."

"Not too far," Pastor Billings says. He sits in the chair beside the bed, pulling it around some so that he can look at Lloyd from a better angle. "We came over from First Baptist Church."

A bit puzzled now, Lloyd comments, "Well, that's my church, but I don't recognize you fellas. You must be new."

"Somewhat, I suppose."

"Although, I have been trapped here in this house for some time now, so I guess that explains it," Mr. Bishop concedes.

"Dear, are you going to be all right with these gentlemen for a while? I shouldn't be too long," Mrs. Bishop says.

"Yes, I'll be fine. I don't suppose they have come all this way to hurt an old man like me," he quips.

"Well, OK then. I will be home in a bit," she says, and kisses him on the forehead before turning to leave with Mrs. Billings and Allison.

Da Juan settles in to a chair on the opposite side of the bed from Pastor Billings. "Are you new to the church also?" Lloyd asks, looking Da Juan over from top to bottom. "You must be. I'm sure I would remember you. That's a lot of hair, young man."

Neither Mr. Billings nor Da Juan can hold back a laugh, and that makes Lloyd laugh as well. "I actually just came over this week with my friends. We came to help the pastor out with a few things."

"Well, that's very nice. I'm sure he will appreciate it," Lloyd says. "Who is the pastor nowadays?"

"That's him over there," Da Juan says, pointing to Pastor Billings.

Lloyd, surprised, looks over and sees the pastor. "Oh, that's right; that lady told me that. I'm sorry, I forgot."

"That lady? You mean your wife," Da Juan says.

Matter-of-factly, with a stern look on his face, Lloyd replies, "She is not my wife. She treats me fine, but she won't let me go home. I want to go home to see my wife."

Da Juan, taken aback, looks over to Pastor Billings, who looks back and mouths the words, *It's OK.*

"Would you two take me home?" Lloyd asks. "It can show you where it is."

Pastor Billings, not wanting to disappoint Lloyd, but also not wanting to upset Annie, reluctantly agrees. "I guess I can take you for a drive, and see what we see. Would that be okay?"

Lloyd is hoping for more of a commitment, but accepts the deal. Da Juan and Pastor Billings help Lloyd to the car and into the front passenger seat. Da Juan sits in the back, and Pastor Billings drives. This is not the first time Pastor Billings has taken Lloyd for a drive to search for his home, so he knows what to expect. Driving slowly enough for Lloyd to look things over, the pastor takes all the routes that he knows he should. Every turn is approved by Lloyd, yet he is still dissatisfied. Frustration grows in his eyes, and he lets out a soft sigh. "I don't understand," he says, becoming wearier as each word comes out. "It used to be near here. It all looks familiar, but it's not quite what I'm looking for." He has them circle the area several times, but cannot find what he I looking for. "I guess you should just take me back to that other house," Lloyd says, unable to mask the utter despair that has set in.

"I'm sorry, Lloyd. I know you are upset," Pastor Billings says. "It is a pretty day, though. Would you like to sit in the park for a while, and feel the warm air?"

"I suppose that would be all right, for a little while," he replies. "Thank you for trying to help me."

"You're welcome, Lloyd," Pastor Billings says, trying to hide the tears rolling down his cheeks.

Da Juan has been pondering this entire turn of events from the back seat, not quite sure what to make of it all. Questions fill his mind, but he dares not ask them until he has a chance to speak privately with the pastor.

When they reach the park, Da Juan helps Pastor Billings get Lloyd situated in his wheel chair in a good spot to watch the flurry of summertime activities that the park has to offer. There are mothers and young children on the playground equipment. Dogs are chasing balls and Frisbees that their owners have thrown. Women and men of all ages are running at different paces all over the park, checking their heart rate and calorie burn on their wristband monitors. The two men sit and talk with Mr. Bishop, pointing out squirrels and birds and such, which bring smiles to his face every time. He doesn't get out of the house often, because it is difficult for Annie to tend to him away from home now, so his mind is in sensory overload, like a child walking into an amusement park.

After an hour or so, Da Juan notices that Lloyd has drifted off to sleep, so he takes the opportunity to gets some answers. "OK, so why did he get so upset? What was he looking for?"

Pastor Billings looks down to make sure Lloyd is asleep, then replies, "He was remembering a house that he and Annie lived in when they were younger. The house is still there and we went by it several times, but because the highways have changed, as well as some other landmarks, he didn't recognize it.

Next Summer

This has happened before; he is always disappointed, but I take him because he would become very belligerent if I didn't. He feels trapped all the time. He feels he is forced to live in a house he doesn't belong in, with a person he doesn't know. That's why I brought him here, just to give him a good event for the day."

"Oh man, that's horrible," Da Juan says, looking back at Lloyd.

Across town, the ladies are finishing brunch at one of Annie's favorite restaurants. Sitting outside at a table on the street, they enjoy the warm air. They have laughed a lot, and even cried a little. Mrs. Billings has updated her on happenings at church, and Allison has told her of the group's summer mission trip. "That sounds like the most wonderful time. Oh, I just know that my Lloyd would have loved to be a part of something like that. He always wanted to be remembered for some grand thing," Annie says, and looks off into the distance. A moment passes with no words before Annie begins again. "When he was first diagnosed with dementia, he was so disappointed that he had never accomplished something of that magnitude."

Allison breaks in to protest. "But he did. He did accomplish something great. You both did," she says. The two ladies look back at her, wondering where she is going with her statement. "How many people can say they have been married for fifty years? It's not that common any more. Most couples can't stand each other after a few years, a decade at most, and find any reason to break up." Mrs. Bishop begins to well up with tears.

"That's right," Mrs. Billings agrees, nodding. "You two have shown everyone you know what real commitment is."

"I guess we never thought of it like that," Annie says, sighing.

"Sister, you have no idea how much of an example you are setting for our church," Mrs. Billings says.

"Well, I really appreciate you saying that, but I don't much feel like an example any more. It's hard. I hate this disease every day, and I hate that it has taken that man from me. He knew me better than anyone but God, and now he doesn't even recognize me. I get angry and fuss—and yes, I even cuss sometimes—and complain to God. Then, when I calm down, I ask Him to forgive me, and thank Him for all the years I had with Lloyd." Annie sits with her face turned away for a moment, weeping quietly. Allison and Mrs. Billings simply being there helps her recover. "In the beginning, it was different. I had to watch it slowly take things from him: how to fix this, or how that works. Our boys would come over and ask him about something, something that he had done a thousand times before, and he would sit there frustrated and tell them he *knew* that he knew how to do it, and that he had done it many times before, but he couldn't remember how to help them. It took away the things that made him proud of his accomplishments. It took away the things that made him who he was."

Now, all three ladies sit there weeping together.

After a few moments, Annie begins to wipe her eyes and clear her throat. "I'm sorry," she apologizes. "This is a good day, a day out with friends. Let's go somewhere cheerful."

"All right, Dear. Where would you like to go?" Mrs. Billings asks, standing from the table and signing the receipt for their meal.

"You know, Lloyd and I used to go to the park a lot on the weekends. Let's go there." She begins to stand, and as she does, she spots a single white feather on the ground under the edge of the table. Picking it up and showing the others, she says. "Lloyd used to always say that feathers reminded him of angels, and that when he saw one it made him feel like one was nearby watching over him." Opening her purse, she continues. "I think I will take it home and show him."

Arriving at the park, Mrs. Billings spots her and her husband's vehicle and points it out to the others. "There's our car, so the guys must be here too." Annie begins to search for them and spots them across the way, Lloyd's head leaning over to one side. At that moment, as if on cue, he wakes. Looking around, he realizes where he is and turns to see who is near. "Pastor, thank you for letting me rest," he says, looking over his shoulder at Pastor Billings.

"Oh, you're welcome, Brother. I hope it was good rest," Pastor Billings replies. Then he pauses to ponder what just happened.

"I do feel a bit better, thank you."

Lloyd begins to look around the park and smiles at all of the people out having a good day. Then he notices a single white feather on the ground beside Da Juan's foot. "Young man, would you hand me that feather, please?" he requests, pointing to the ground.

"What, where?" Da Juan asks, looking down. "Oh, OK." He bends down to pick it up.

The ladies are now walking straight for the guys, and Annie seems to have a bit of a bounce in her step. Lloyd suddenly spots them coming, and he reaches for the pastor. Seeing his movement, Pastor Billings leans over to see what he needs. "Pastor, is that my wife coming towards us?" Lloyd says waving one hand in the ladies' direction.

"I do believe you are right, Lloyd," the pastor replies, patting him on the shoulder.

"Would be all right if we meet them halfway?"

"Let's do it," Pastor Billings agrees. "Da Juan, help me out here," he says, smiling at the young man, who is grinning back at him.

Together, the three head straight for the ladies. The ladies notice the guys moving towards them and smile. When the two groups meet in the middle, Lloyd lifts up his feather to show Annie. "Look what I found, Sweetheart," he says, smiling from ear to ear.

Tears begin to fall from Annie's eyes as she reaches into her purse. Pulling out her feather, she holds it up for Lloyd to see. "I found one, too," she says, smiling through her tears, then leans over to kiss her husband.

Chapter Twenty-Four

It takes a church to build a church

I know, that's powerful stuff, huh? Try watching it unfold in front of you. We were all crying and then smiling, and then crying again. It was one of the best days of my life. We stayed there at the park for just a little while longer before we took them home. Pastor Billings called the Bishops' children and told them that he had an overwhelming feeling that they should all come home immediately and spend the rest of the day with their parents. They did, and thankfully so. Their father was tired and weak, but he recognized everyone. It was as if they hadn't seen each other in years, and at the same time it was as if nothing was wrong at all. A lot of laughing and crying went on, and Lloyd met his newest grandchild, so it was a wonderful time for the Bishop family. I'm sure you probably know where I'm going with this. That was Lloyd's last good day; it was his last day of all, in fact. They stayed up late into the morning, but it was apparent to everyone that something was happening. A little before dawn, Lloyd took his last breath, and then went home to be with the Lord. The whole family sat around his bed with him, so he was not alone at all in his last moments. Everyone knew him, and he knew everyone.

•••••••

Scratch, scratch, scratch. "Man, this drywall sanding is no joke," Joey says, still not happy with his work.

"You got *that* right," Sterling replies. "I feel like Daniel-san, from *The Karate Kid*."

"'Wax on, wax off,'" Joey quotes, moving one hand in circles in one direction, then circling the other in the opposite direction. "You just keep sanding drywall, Daniel-san. You be ready for tournament in no time."

Raul edges over to get into the conversation. "So, which one do you like best?"

"Original, hello," Sterling and Joey both say, looking at him as if it should be understood.

"Yeah, I figured. Just checking," Raul replies.

"How about *The Next Karate Kid*?" Kendra asks as she walks by.

"The one with the girl?" Da Juan interjects.

"I'm gonna pretend you didn't just ask that," Sterling replies.

Kendra pulls herself up into the crane position, mimicking the character in the movie. "Boy, don't make me do it," she warns, a fake threat.

All the boys look at each other for just a second, then burst into laughter.

Kendra pulls herself back down and mocks them even more. "You see, that's why none of you have any girlfriends," she teases, tsk, tsk, tsking her index finger back and forth at them.

"Yep, that about says it all," Allison agrees, walking past. "Oh, and you missed a spot," she says, pointing to a place on the wall.

As the week goes on, the group transforms the church addition they'd been working on into a brand-new church fellowship hall. From sanding to painting to trim work to decorating, they'd worked on every inch of the room. Saturday has arrived, and with all of the inside finished, they turn their efforts to landscaping and other finishing touches outside. As everyone wraps up breakfast, the church pastor stands to speak. "I want to thank you all once again for all of the hard work you've done this week, finishing our church fellowship hall. It has been a long journey for us; we have been working on this for seven years now. We had decided long ago not to take out a loan for this, so we set out to raise money for materials and decided to do the work ourselves. As much as we could, anyway. Your help this week has caught up a project that was several weeks behind schedule, allowing us to open on time for our yearly homecoming dinner." With that, all of the church members present stood with their pastor and clapped for the group. "If you can work with us just one more day, we will finish, and then we will treat you to a wonderful feast."

Everyone has finished breakfast, and now heads out into the hot August morning to work. There are shrubs to plant, flower boxes are being built and then filled, and a gravel walkway from the new addition to the parking lot slowly takes shape. Mulch finds its way around all of the nearby trees; before the grass is mowed, there are several large trees to be planted. All hands are on deck for these large trees, to make sure everything goes smoothly. Jason and Raul push a landscaping dolly with one of the trees on it across the yard, lining it up with hole that has been prepared for it. Renee and Kendra stand ready to help guide it into its new spot. "Dear, can you two scrape the sides of the hole to make it just a bit wider please?" Jason asks.

"Oh, OK," Renee responds. "Allison, while we're doing this, loosen the burlap around the root ball and break open the roots a bit, please."

"On it," Allison replies, springing into action.

Renee and Kendra slice at the edges of the hole with their shovels to widen it.

"Sweetheart, you don't have to work so fast; we're all right," Jason says, as they continue to hold the tree in place.

"Just don't want you guys to hurt yourselves," she responds, scooping out the loose dirt.

As soon as the ladies finish the prep work, they reach up to help the guys lower the tree into place. "Yay!" Renee exclaims, clapping her hands as they pull away. "That looks great."

They all rake the loose soil back into the hole and reach for the water hose to top it off.

"That looks so good." Renee says, sweat pouring down her pale skin.

"Dear, are you all right?" Jason asks. "You're looking very pale." Stepping around the tree, he studies her face with growing alarm.

Taking a deep breath and wiping her forehead, she replies, "I'm fi–" She collapses to the ground mid-word, just before his outstretched arms reach her.

"Renee!" he cries, diving to the ground. "Guys, call nine-one-one."

Allison, Kendra, and Raul drop down to their knees to try to help. "What can we do?" Kendra asks.

"Something cool! Get a wash cloth, a cool, damp wash cloth," Jason says frantically.

"I'm going, I'm going," Allison says, jumping to her feet.

Raul dials 911 on his cellphone.

Chapter Twenty-Five

Would you like an envelope for that?

Pretty horrible way to leave you, huh? Renee gave us quite the scare, didn't she? Especially when you consider that she is pregnant. You didn't forget about that, did you? I didn't think so. Well, we had her sitting up and sipping some water before the EMTs arrived, but of course they went through the whole protocol. They believed she had simply pushed herself too hard in the heat, but they took her to the hospital anyway to make sure, and to check on the baby. For safety's sake, she stayed the night and was back with us in the morning. And yes, the baby was fine.

We all decided to take a water break after the ambulance left and then went on to finish the day and the project. With the new church fellowship hall finally complete, the fine cooks of the church took over and prepared a feast worthy to dedicate a castle. Mr. Fisher was the guest speaker. Renee and Jason were with us, and everyone had a great day. I know, kinda boring huh? Sorry, not everything can be edge-of-your-seat stuff. After Renee scaring us, we were looking forward to a quiet last week anyway.

••••••••

"We're getting close to the city. Do you want to stop at a bank now, or wait until we are back in town?" Mr. Fisher asks as he drives.

"Let me see where the nearest one is," Jason replies, tapping on his phone for information. "Looks like there's one just off of exit twenty-three."

"OK, that's coming up soon; we're at twenty-five now," Tim replies.

Tim puts on his right turn signal and after checking that it's clear, eases into the right lane. As they approach the exit ramp, red and blue flashing lights take over the area. An accident on the overpass has traffic held up, and the off ramp is full. "Do we still want to take this exit, Jason?" Tim asks.

Looking up to see the mess, Renee says, "We can just find one in the city, can't we?"

"Yeah, that's fine. We certainly want to avoid any drama today."

Smiling, Renee comes back with a quick comment. "So, does that mean the movie we're going to see has to be a comedy?"

Reaching over to hold her hand, Jason replies. "OK, we want to avoid any *real-life* drama. Is that more precise?" he teases, grinning at her.

She giggles and pecks him on the cheek.

"OK, we will keep on keepin' on, then," Tim says. "Can you guys see how close the nearest bank is to the museum we're stopping at?"

"Sure. I'm on it," Tim says, already tapping away at his phone once again. "Actually, there's one just three blocks from our stop. I can walk from there."

"Excellent! Thank you. We should only be about another forty-five minutes," Tim says, keeping his eyes on the road and hands on the wheel.

•••••

Tim pulls the bus into the museum parking lot, and sits back in his seat for just a moment to relax. "So, what's the plan, Renee? Do we eat first, or go straight in to the museum?" he asks, turning to see the whole group beginning to come alive.

"I think eat first, then museum," she answers.

"OK. Well, let me slip by the bank real quick. I just wanted to pull out some cash so the guys could pick up something for themselves without having to come to us for everything," Jason says "I shouldn't be long."

"Mind if we tag along?" Sterling asks.

"Yeah, gotta get these legs moving again," Da Juan says, bouncing to his feet.

"Sure, let's go. You guys want to scope out a place to eat?" Jason says as he pecks his wife on the cheek.

"OK, I'll text you what we find."

This being their last week, and not being expected at the church until tomorrow, the group plans to have a fun afternoon of sightseeing and then maybe a movie. Renee and the group head off to find a place for lunch while Jason and the boys make their way to the bank.

"After you, kind sirs," Da Juan says, bowing as he holds the door open for

Sterling and Jason.

Walking through with his head held high and putting on fake airs, in his best British accent, Sterling replies, "Why thank you, my good man."

Jason simply nods as he walks through.

"Indubitably," Da Juan adds and follows them in.

As they make their way in, they are greeted by a young man in a ball cap and dark sunglasses. He has a pistol pointed straight at them, and a lifeless expression on his face.

The three guys start to back up once they see what is in front of them, but the voice attached to the gun speaks up. "No, no, no. Come on in here, and get on the floor."

Reluctantly, they ease their way across the floor and sit with others already there.

"I told you to get that door locked so no one else would come in," another voice with a gun yells from across the room. "Hurry it up, you idiot," this other voice seems to belong to the leader of this group, with a third gun over near the people on the floor. The two followers are pacing back and forth, obviously very nervous. The leader has his gun pointed at the only teller left behind the counter. She is a young, pretty, small woman, and was picked because she seemed to be not quite sure of herself. "Now, let's get back to the task at hand," the leader says to the young woman, looking at her name plate. "Jessica; look at me, and put your hands above the counter." She complies without a word. "If you touch that silent alarm, I will bite off those pretty little fingers one by one. Do you believe me, Jessica?"

She nods her reply.

"Now let's quickly get me what I want, so I can leave you fine folks with all your digits," The leader continues. Around the counter he goes, taking the teller with him to the vault door.

The other two gunmen walk close to each other to talk. "This will all be over soon, Russell. Just keep your cool and we will be outta here in a minute," one gunman whispers to the other.

"OK. I just have a bad feeling, Eric. Plus, Smyth is always yelling at me. Why does he hate me so much?" Russell asks.

"He hates everybody. He only tolerates me 'cuz I'm his brother," Eric replies empathetically.

Jason, noticing the two gunmen talking and not paying close attention to the hostages, takes out his cell phone, and quickly texts Renee.

At bank…being held up by 3 men with guns…call police…we are OK.

Eric and Russell begin closing the bank door and window blinds. Da Juan and Sterling are sitting in front of Jason, in hopes that the gunmen won't notice what he is doing, which they do not. Once he is finished, they all breathe a bit easier.

Jason, of course, is second-guessing the decision to come to this bank rather than wait in traffic at the other one. Should he be doing something, or just wait to let the whole thing play itself out? How would he ever face the boys' parents if something happened to them? His brow furls and his eyes scan the whole room repeatedly, looking for an idea, any idea.

Da Juan sits quietly, looking at all the scared faces: bank employees, customers, and even the two gunmen. He wonders what in particular they came to steal. Is it something sophisticated, like bearer bonds, as if they were in a thriller movie? Or is it simply bags of cash they're after? Then, his eyes finish circling the room and land on Sterling, and the silly look on his face. "What on earth are you finding so amusing during all of this?" Da Juan whispers.

Sterling looks over at him and replies, "I was just thinking how odd it is to be sitting in the middle of a bank robbery, watching the bank commercials on the TVs."

Da Juan looks at him for a second, puzzled, and Sterling motions toward one of the screens. Turning to look, the thought of what Sterling said finally catches up to Da Juan, and he lets out a giggle. The gunmen turn to see the grins on the boys faces. "Shut up!" Eric screams across the room.

Russell moves quickly to the boys. "Look, you guys don't wanna make this hard. We're tryin' to get out of here quickly, but Smy—I mean, the other guy is the boss, and he ain't as easygoin' as we are," he says, motioning downward with his hands. "So keep it down."

"Let's not agitate the situation, guys," Jason says quietly, leaning in to them. "This is the real deal."

"Sorry, Jason," Da Juan offers.

"Yeah, we didn't mean to upset them," Sterling adds.

•••••••

Walking out of the museum, the group heads back to the bus to wait for Jason and the guys. Renee hears her cell phone chirp, announcing a new text message, and pulls it from her pocket. Pulling up the screen she can hardly believe what Jason has sent. Stopping in her tracks, she looks at her screen, puzzled. The group carries on several steps before they notice she has stopped. "Is everything all right, Renee?" Tim asks, turning back to see her concerned look.

"No. No, it's definitely *not* okay," she replies, still staring at her screen.

"Guys, wait," Tim speaks above the chatter. The group all stops and turns back to see tears in Renee's eyes. "Renee what is it? You're scaring me," Tim says, and walks back to her. The group all gathers around her.

Looking up in fear, she shows them the text message. "Jason and the boys are stuck in the middle of a bank robbery," she says, her voice now very shaky.

"What!?" says about half the group, but only gasps come from the rest.

"Let me see," Tim says, and reads it over for himself. "He wouldn't—" He stops himself as he sees her head shaking. "Of course not. I know he wouldn't joke about something like this. OK, he says for us to call the police. You guys try to flag down an officer if you see one, and I will call nine-one-one."

Everyone takes off in different directions, trying to find a police car. Everyone except Allison hurries away; she stays with Renee. "It's gonna be all right," she reassures Renee, rubbing her shoulder.

"I can't lose him. I've waited too long for this," Renee says frantically.

"Let's go back to the bus." Allison gently takes her arm and begins to lead her in that direction. "It's gonna be all right."

They start walking back towards the bus when Renee remembers her phone. "My phone! I need my phone. He may text again," she says, looking at Allison as if she needed help.

"Don't worry," Allison says. "Kendra!" she yells back to the group, now forming again around Mr. Fisher. "Grab Renee's cellphone and come with us!"

Kendra quickly gets the phone from Mr. Fisher, and runs to catch up. "Got it," she says, almost out of breath.

The three finally make it back to the bus and sit down. Unknowingly, they walk past guardian angel Thaniel, sitting in the driver seat. "I can't lose him now. I can't raise this baby alone," Renee continues, frantically. "And what about Da Juan and Sterling? What if something happens to them? How will I face their parents?"

"They will be fine," Kendra tries her hand at calming Renee. "They're together." "Yeah; I mean, who would you rather he be with, than those two? They're golden. Everything always works out for them," Allison adds.

"Yeah, but that has to end eventually," Renee retorts.

"Renee, we have to believe they will be fine," Kendra says, holding Renee's hand.

"Of course they will," Allison continues, nodding slowly.

"Stop saying that! You don't know that!" Renee snaps, pulling her hand back "We can't be sure of that."

Thaniel begins to whisper the word *pray*, over and over. Allison looks beside the driver seat of the bus and sees something on the floor. "What is that?" she says, reaching to pick it up. "Look, Renee; it's a feather," she says, holding it up. "Remember, the Bishops?"

Renee looks in amazement at the find and then back at the girls. "We need to start praying."

Chapter Twenty-Six

What are we gonna do now?

Sirens outside the bank break the relative calm that has settled inside. Eric and Russell look at each other in fear, not knowing what would be worse: the police arresting them, or Smyth's wrath. Right on cue, their fears are realized. Smyth comes striding from the vault room in an explosion of verbal obscenities. "What is that sound?!" he screams, dragging Jessica behind him by the arm. "We could have been done and outta here, but now look what we have." Furious, he slings her to the floor near the other hostages and paces back and forth near the counter. In a fit of rage, he points his gun at Jessica as he rushes back to her. "Hit the button anyway, didn't you?" he screams.

"No! No, I didn't. I promise, please..." she pleads, recoiling in fear.

Reaching for her arm again and jerking her to her feet, he pins her against the wall and puts the gun right up to her forehead. As she breathes heavily and whimpers under his attack, he screams at her again. "Lie to me again! I *dare* you."

Jankiel and Haniel are watching the scene unfold, and have been discussing how to best handle themselves. Jankiel whispers behind Jason that he should stand up and confess.

"She's not lying," Smyth hears. He looks over his shoulder, then turns to see from whom this insolence comes.

Jessica is so relieved that Smyth has turned away from her she almost relaxes too much, and has to catch herself so she doesn't fall.

"And just how do you know she's not lying?" Smyth says as he turns to face Jason, now standing in front of him.

"I know because I did it," Jason replies.

"OK, either you're really stupid, or—you're really stupid," Smyth says now pointing the gun in Jason's face. "But I'll bite, Cowboy. So, tell me; what did you do? Did you make your way over in front of these idiots and push that button?"

"I texted," Jason says.

Smyth begins breathing heavily as his countenance falls further. Looking over Jason's shoulder, he stares at his brother. "What were you doing? You two find yourselves a bit too busy to watch these people while I get the money?"

"I don't know how he did it, Smyth," Eric says, shaking his head.

"Thanks a lot, Moron! You wanna go ahead and tell everyone *all* of our names?" Smyth barks.

Looking down at the floor, Eric responds, "You got me all messed up."

"Oh, I'm *gonna* mess you up, Little Brother. And your loser friend, too," he says, but then turns his focus back to Jason. "I'm not done with you yet. I was almost ready to grab and go, but no; you wanted to be a hero, and take me down. Well, you know, sometimes heroes don't make it to the end of the movie."

"Smyth, no!" Russell blurts out.

"Stop saying my name, Russell!" he screams back. "What, you wanna be the one to not make it to the end?" Smyth says, pointing his gun toward Russell.

Russell, startled, raises his gun to point it at Smyth. Eric's body jerks, and he raises his gun toward Smyth as well. "Oh, so now you're on his side?" Smyth yells to his brother, which makes him turn to point his weapon toward Russell instead. Confused, he looks back and forth between the two.

"No one needs to die here today," Jason says. He glances at Da Juan and Sterling, who are shocked by how quickly the whole situation has spiraled out of control.

"Cowboy, if anyone dies today, it's gonna be *you*. So, you need to shut up," Smyth snaps, pointing his gun at Jason once more. "What do ya think of that?"

Jason stands silently for a second, half scared and half furious. At that moment, Haniel rests his hand on Jason's shoulder, giving him strength to speak, and whispers in his ear. Jason closes his eyes, shakes his head, and opens his eyes again to reply to his captor. "I don't want to die today; I have a wife who is pregnant with our first child. But I'm a Christian, so I know where I'll go if I do die today. Can you say that?"

Smyth is taken aback by this comment and relaxes his stance a bit. "*What did you just say to me?*"

"I said, I know where I'll go if I die today. How about you? There are police outside waiting for a chance to come in. What if your day doesn't end the way you want?" Jason says.

As if Jason planned it, everyone hears a bull horn outside come to life. "This is the police. We know you have hostages. You need to let them go before you make a huge mistake."

Smyth looks off into space for a second, then back to Jason. "Fine, you're saved for now. Get back over there, and sit down and shut up."

•••••••

Two hours later, everyone is still in the bank. Smyth has been talking to the police while trying to figure his way out of this mess. Eric has been tasked with finishing the money gathering, and Russell is watching over the hostages. Regretting ever having met Smyth, Russell paces back and forth, mumbling to himself.

"Russell, you don't have to hang in with this guy. You haven't done anything too bad yet," Da Juan says quietly.

Russell turns to look at him and thinks for a moment about what he said. "Yeah, like I can just walk outta here, free, today," he says. "Just leave me alone before he hears you."

"C'mon man, you gotta know this guy is not looking out for you," Sterling adds. "We've been listening to how he talks to you. Heck, even to his own brother."

"Yeah. I mean, look at our leader. He doesn't talk to us like that. He even stood up to that jerk when it could've gotten him killed," Da Juan says.

"Well, that was just stupid," Russell says, running his hand through his hair and huffing in frustration. "Do you really believe all that stuff?"

"You mean, about going to heaven and being sure of it? Yeah, we do," Sterling whispers.

"You can believe, too. It's for you as much as us," Da Juan adds.

"I mean, I see my mom, and she believes in God and stuff, but that stuff is for good people. I'm not a good person. I wouldn't be here if I was," Russell says, taking a deep breath and remembering his mother.

"That's where you're wrong, Russell. The Bible says that there is none good but God. None of us is really good," Sterling continues.

"You sayin' my mom is not good?" Russell demands sternly.

Waving his hands back and forth in front of himself as if wiping off a chalk board, Sterling says, "That's not what I mean. I believe you when you say your mom is good, but compared to God, none of us are good. We all have mistakes and sins of some sort, either now or in the past. God is perfect, though, in every way. His thoughts, his actions, his everything. We really can't compare to that."

Russell thinks on that for a second as Da Juan adds, "That's the thing; none of us are as good as God. We can't be. We have a sick nature. We are all broken at heart, but even though God knew that, he still put his own presence into flesh. His own son was put into a human body to live this life so he could understand all that we endure, living as broken people in a cursed world. He lived it perfectly, and then sacrificed his life to die the death that we all deserve. To pay the price for our sins."

"Yeah, and I bet if you asked your mom about this, she would tell you the same thing. You can believe in God's son, too. You can believe in Jesus, and you can say like us that you know where you will go when it's your time to die."

"Are you gonna stand there and talk all day with your best buds, or are you with me?" Smyth screams across the room staring straight at Russell.

"C'mon Smyth, ease up! He's not doing anything wrong," Eric says, trying to smooth things over.

"You know what? How 'bout *no*? I'm tryin' to get us outta here. Now, if you and loser over there wanna stay, well then, be my guest," Smyth replies sarcastically.

"Look, he don't mean no harm. He's just trying to get through this," Eric pleads.

Looking back and forth between Russell and Eric, Smyth finishes the tie. "Don't care what he's tryin' to do. I'm not babysittin' you anymore. Do what you're told, or go back to your loser mom. Maybe she can change your diapers for ya."

"Don't talk about my mother. You leave her outta this," Russell screams, his face turning red and his eyes welling up.

Guardian angels, Jankiel and Haniel realize the situation has come to a boiling point. "What do we do?" Jankiel says.

"There isn't much we *can* do. You know that," Haniel replies. "You are right though; this doesn't look good. You stay close to Russell, and I'll stay with Eric."

Jankiel nods in agreement and quickly moves into place.

"Maybe she's part of this already," Smyth says smugly. "If she wasn't such a loser, you wouldn't be one."

Pointing his gun at Smyth with tears streaming down his face, Russell continues his warning, albeit visibly shaken. "I *told* you to leave her out of this. I'm only here trying to make some money to help her out."

Smyth now raises his gun quickly to match Russell's. "Such a good little momma's boy, aren't you?"

Da Juan, afraid for Russell jumps up out of reflex and stands in front of him, holding him back with one hand and pointing at Smyth with the other. "All right, please let him alone and go back to talking to the police."

Sterling also jumps up. Tugging at Da Juan's shirt, he says, "What are you doing, Bro? Come sit back down."

"Yeah, listen to your friend, Punk. Sit down before you get hurt. This ain't your business," Smyth snarls.

Outside, the police can hear the screaming inside and realize the distraction is giving them an opportunity. The captain sends two men close enough to the building to see in through cracks between the blinds and window frames. They quickly move into place to try to assess the situation inside.

Oblivious to the movement outside, the argument continues. "I'm just trying to help Russell." Da Juan replies to his friend. "I don't want to see him get hurt."

"I don't want to see either of you get hurt," Sterling replies.

Eric begins to tug at Smyth's shirt. "Come on, Smyth. Leave him alone, and get us out of here," he says.

"Oh, so now you're worried about the *plan* finally, instead of your loser friend," Smyth says, pushing him away. "Tell him to put his gun down and I will."

"Russell, put your gun down, Man," Eric pleads. "It's gonna be okay."

"Yeah, Loser, put your gun down before I send you back to mommy in a body bag," Smyth continues his verbal abuse.

Russell leans around to the right side of Da Juan to respond. "I'm not telling you again, *leave her out of this!*" he screams, wiping his eyes with his left arm, still pointing the gun at Smyth with his right.

The two police officers watching the scene inside through the blinds call for a few more men, wanting them closer to be in place if an opportunity to burst in presented itself.

"No, I'm not telling you again. Drop the gun, or I'm shootin' you," Smyth replies.

"Smyth, cut it out. Put the gun down," Eric demands.

"Sit down, Da Juan," Jason calls out, as Sterling pulls at his sleeves.

"Put your gun away, Russell," Da Juan pleads.

"Not 'til he does," Russell replies, stepping away from Da Juan. "I'm tired of him talking about my mother."

"I don't care what you're tired of. I'm done with you," Smyth warns. "Last time I'm gonna say it. Put it down."

"No. You first."

Smyth aims his gun. Da Juan watches as Smyth begins to squeeze the trigger. Everything seems to be in slow motion as Eric pushes Smyth backward. Angel Haniel gives an added push to help Eric. The stress from the struggle throws Smyth off balance just as he finishes the squeeze on the trigger. The bullet comes flying out in a thunderous roar and a puff of smoke. Da Juan pulls away from Sterling and dives onto Russell, aided by angel Jankiel, who notices the speed and trajectory of the bullet. The shove causes Da Juan to move Russell out of the path of the bullet, but he himself does not elude it. The bullet tears through Da Juan's chest, just beneath the right clavicle. The sound of the gunshots alerts the police, who decide to wait no longer before firing tear gas grenades through the front plate glass windows. Following the smoke, the police storm in and quickly pounce on Smyth, who was about to fire a second time.

Chapter Twenty-Seven

Not another trip to the hospital

As the smoke begins to clear Smyth, Eric, and Russell are cuffed and led out to the police cruisers. For most of the hostages, the ordeal is over—but for three of them, it is just beginning. Da Juan lies on the bank floor in a puddle of his own blood. His moans are only outdone by Sterling's screams for an ambulance. "What is *wrong* with you? Why would you *do* that?" Sterling cries.

"I couldn't let him shoot Russell," Da Juan struggles to say between groans. "I think he really is a good guy."

"That's all well and good, but you're supposed to dive *under* the bullet, not into it" Sterling says, trying to lighten the mood a bit. "Haven't you learned anything from all the movies we've watched together?"

"Ungh. Don't make me laugh, Dummy. This really hurts," Da Juan says. He turns his head and looks off into the distance.

"What is it? What are looking at? Is it a bright light? Come on, Dude, don't go into the light. Stay here with me."

"It's not a light, Bro. I think it's a feather. Can you get it for me?" Da Juan struggles to ask.

"What?" Sterling asks. He turns to look for the feather. "Oh, OK." He gets it and brings it back to Da Juan, just as the paramedics arrive. "Why do want this feather, Bro?"

Da Juan, breathing heavily, responds, "I'll tell ya later, Bro. I'm not feeling too..." Da Juan passes out and the paramedics work to revive him, asking Sterling and Jason to step back to give them room.

•••••••

Renee and the others hurry over to the bank to pick up Jason and Sterling, then they all rush to the emergency room. Everyone files into the emergency room, quickly filling it. The attendant behind the counter begins to be alarmed when she sees the great number of people coming in all at once. "Are all of you together? How many of you are hurt?" she asks, hoping for the best.

"We are all together, but none of us are hurt," Mr. Fisher replies, prompting a confused look from the attendant. "We need to check on a member of our group, please."

"A member of your group?"

"Yes, he came in with a gunshot wound."

"Did you shoot him?

"What?! No!"

"Self-inflicted?"

"No! He was at the bank across town when it was robbed."

"Did you just get here?" Sterling breaks in to ask. "Have you seriously not heard that a patient was shot at a bank robbery?"

"No. I was actually just messing with you guys," she replies, dryly.

Tim and Sterling turn to look at each other for a moment in confusion, then turn back to her. "Oh, I get it; don't get gunshot patients that often, and you couldn't help yourself?"

"Well, you'd be surprised," she replies, the same serious look on her face. "What's the name?"

"Noble. Da Juan Noble," Tim replies.

She begins to peck on her keyboard, but abruptly stops. "Could you spell that?"

Tim and Sterling, again share a glance before Tim answers. "N-o-b-l-e."

"No, not that one. The first name," she says.

"Geez-Louise. It's D-a-j-u-a-n." Sterling spells impatiently. "We do have the right hospital, don't we?"

"Oh, there it is. Yes, you have the right place. Give me a moment to see what I can find out," she responds, then leaves the desk to check.

"What do you think, Jason? Is that good or bad? If he was OK, would they just tell us? Does that mean he's in a bad way?" Sterling asks Jason, who just walked up to the front.

Jason turns and spots Allison looking his way, and motions with his eyes for her to come help with Sterling. "I don't know, Buddy. We just need to wait and see what they have to say before we get all bent out of shape."

Allison steps up close to Sterling and takes his arm. "Come on, Sterling; let's sit over here for a few minutes."

"All right, but only until they come out with word on how he is," Sterling responds as they walk over to a nearby row of chairs.

After a few moments, the woman behind the desk returns. Now, she has someone with her. "Hi folks," the new person says. "I am one of the nurses who has been working on your friend..." Looking at the chart, she tries to pronounce his name. "Da Juan."

Everyone gathers around to hear the news. "Is he all right? Does he need blood? One of us is bound to match. How about a kidney? He can have one of mine." Sterling, wearing his fear on his sleeves and everywhere else as well, asks a barrage of questions.

"Sterling, he was shot in the shoulder, not the kidney. Just relax, and let's hear what she has to say," Allison says, still holding his arm.

"OK, here's what I can tell you. I just spoke with his parents on the phone, who, as you know, are on their way. He suffered a gunshot wound to the upper right chest, which punctured his right lung. That's the bad news," she says, stopping to catch her breath. "He's in surgery now, critical but stable. I would like to move everyone to a waiting room on the surgical floor, if that would be all right. Mr. and Mrs. Noble have been instructed as to where to find you when they arrive."

Chapter Twenty-Eight

Memories aren't enough

With the whole group upstairs in the surgical waiting room, there isn't much room for anyone else, but they are being as quiet as a large group can be. After some prayer time, there isn't a dry eye in the room. Renee notices that the usually upbeat Sterling is not at all himself, and understandably so—but she still wants to try to bring him around. "I know you're scared. I get that, but you and Da Juan are the leaders of this group, and he needs you right now," she says quietly, leaning in close beside him. "We need to turn this room around. I have seen too many times when things didn't feel right, and who was it that came to the rescue? Da Juan and Sterling, of course. So while he's down, you're gonna have to carry the torch alone. We all just prayed, and we believe that God hears prayer and is able to raise him up for us. The rest is in God's hands."

"I know, Renee. I do believe. It's just hard right now," he replies with a downcast expression.

"I know it's hard. That's why they're called trials," she responds. "But you can do this."

"Well, what is it that I should do, exactly?" he asks.

"Just let the Lord speak to you, and then follow what He says," Renee replies. Then she stands up, pats him on the shoulder, and walks back over to sit with Jason.

Sterling sits for a few moments with his eyes closed, praying. When he opens his eyes, he looks over to Renee and nods. Standing up, he clears his throat and begins to speak. "All right, I'm done with this. We need some positive thoughts around this place, and we need 'em right now."

Kendra leans over to Allison. "I didn't realize it was so bad in here."

Allison smiles. "I think maybe it just needs to get better for Sterling."

Kendra nods.

Next Summer

"We need positive thoughts, so why don't we all think of good times with Da Juan to pull us through this time of waiting?" Sterling continues.

Raul walks up with some snacks from the vending machine. As he is handing them out, Joey begins to chuckle. "What's so funny?" Allison asks.

He smiles. "Nothing, it's just... I saw the pudding."

"Pudding?" Renee asks, walking up a bit closer.

"Yeah, it was a..." he says, pausing to think. He turns to Raul, Joey, and Sterling. "Guys, do you remember the day he tried to rig up that pudding for Sterling?"

"Oh man, that was hilarious," Sterling recalls.

"Guys, help me move the waiting room chairs into a circle so everyone can hear. Sort of like a campfire story-telling session, just without the fire," Mr. Fisher says, as he begins moving chairs.

••••••

"Hi, guys. Come on in," Mrs. Noble says. "Da Juan is at the back door, setting up something that I'm sure I don't want to know about."

Raul and Joey look at each other and grin, shrugging their shoulders.

"Please tell him for me that as long as no one gets hurt and he cleans up after himself, then we don't have a problem. But if he does not, then..." she says, dragging her thumb across under her chin to signify that he will be in for it.

"Will do, Mrs. N." "

Yes Ma'am, thank you."

As they come closer to the back of the house, they can hear the sounds of Da Juan working at a fever pitch to create another masterpiece of a trap. "Dude, what are you doing this time?" Joey asks.

"Yeah, your mom said to tell you to make sure you clean up, or it's lights out for you," Raul added, snickering

"She said it's light out?" Da Juan asks.

"No, she actually just made the whole knife at the throat reference, but however you wanna take it."

Looking his work over one last time, he says, "It's worth it though. This is gonna be great."

"OK, we can see you're rockin' the whole tipping-bucket classic, but what's inside?" Joey asks, his eyes following the string through its pathway, back to the bucket perched above the mudroom door.

Pointing to the trash can in the corner, Da Juan says, "Check out the trash can."

Joey turns to look at the trash can, then back to Da Juan and then to Raul. He walks over to the can and steps on the pedal, opening the lid. Looking inside, his eyes widen and he says. reverently, "*Dude.* That's a whole lot of chocolate pudding."

Da Juan nods and smiles. "That's right. It's gonna be a thing of beauty," he says smugly.

"Man, you guys are crazy," Raul says, leaning over to see the empty pudding boxes in the trash can. "I don't know how you two come up with this stuff."

"Hey, I see Sterling coming out his back door," Joey announces, tapping Da Juan on the back.

"OK, places, everyone. It's time for the main event," Da Juan says, grinning. "I told him to come over at ten, so he's right on time. Everything is perfect."

The three boys hide around the corner and wait patiently for Sterling to cross the yard and make his way to the back door.

Sterling steps up to the back door and turns the knob, but the screen door is locked, so he rings the doorbell.

"Come on in, Bro," Da Juan hollers from his hiding spot.

"Door's locked, Dude," Sterling replies, looking in the window.

Da Juan, out of reflex, runs to the door and turns the knob to open it. Just as he is pulling back on the door, Joey and Raul yell, "*Noo!*"

It's too late.

Hearing their voices, Da Juan turns to see them as he continues pulling back on the door. Just then the soupy pudding mix pours from the bucket overhead, covering Da Juan's head and dripping down his shirt.

Sterling, not expecting this turn of events, jumps back a step, but then realizes what has happened and bursts into laughter. Raul and Joey wince and recoil as they both exclaim, "Ooh!" Then they too burst into laughter. Sterling is now jumping up and down and clapping, as Da Juan turns to face him and accept defeat by his own hands. Hanging his head, he finally unlocks the screen door to let Sterling in.

Still laughing as he steps inside, Sterling says, "Got yourself *good* this time. Better than I could have."

As Da Juan steps back to let Sterling in, Joey and Raul come closer, still laughing. Raul is cackling almost uncontrollably. "Dude, you–look–like–a–chocolate-covered–ice–cream cone," he says, gasping for air.

Chapter Twenty-Nine

What do condiments have to do with anything?

"That was hilarious, and he really did look like an ice cream cone," Joey says.

"I know; chocolate pudding dripping everywhere. It took us a good while to get that mudroom cleaned up," Raul adds.

Smiling, Sterling continues. "Don't forget how long it took him to get all that pudding out of his hair. Yep, not all of his master plans work out right."

"Well, I remember one of *your* master plans that didn't work out quite right, Sterling," Allison says, waving a pointed finger at him.

"Oh yeah, last summer," Kendra joins in, smiling at Sterling. "What do you call that thing?"

Sitting back in his seat and trying to play it off, Sterling says. "We don't need to bring that one up."

"Yes, we do," Allison retorts.

"OK, I *have* to hear this one," Renee proclaims.

"I remember now," Kendra says, excitedly.

"Don't say it," Sterling pleads.

Allison and Kendra look at each other, then blurt it out in unison. "The gateway to a magical summer evening."

•••••••

"Hey, Bro; I'm here," Da Juan calls out, walking across the lawn to Sterling, who is working feverishly. "I've come to save the day."

"The day *needs* saving," Sterling says. He stops his work long enough to hug his friend. "My masterpiece is done, but it's sure heavy."

"Well, let's go."

The two teens walk into the garage and Da Juan looks at the contraption before him with a combination of awe and utter confusion. "I'm feelin' something, Bro, but I don't know what."

"Don't worry; it'll make sense soon enough," Sterling responds as he bends to pick up his side of the invention.

They carry it across the yard to the spot where Sterling has the rest of his materials sitting. "OK, right here," he says, then works to add decorative camouflage to his work. "Now hand me the water hose."

"So, what is this thing?" Da Juan asks, as he hands Sterling the hose.

Attaching the hose, Sterling steps back and admires his work. "This is a perfect day for this. Summertime, no school, and it's Friday night, so no church in the morning. It'll be great. Wanna turn on the water?"

"Are you gonna let me in on it?" Da Juan asks, turning on the water.

"I figured you'd get it by now." Sterling walks around to the opening of the contraption, which is positioned near the opening of the back yard, leading to a view of the whole area. "This is the gateway to a magical summer evening!" he proclaims, pointing to the sign overhead.

"Yeah, about that... Dude, I'm not feelin' it."

"Well, when an unsuspecting guest steps through..." Sterling says, and then runs through as fast as he can, activating the machine, which shoots cold water from several openings all around the archway. "Voila!"

"Dude, that's awesome! I can't wait to see whose gonna get it first," Da Juan says, wringing his hands together like an evil genius from a movie.

Moments later, just as the group is arriving, there is another arrival.

"What's that sound?" Sterling asks, looking in the direction of the street.

"It's the ice cream man. We passed him on the way in," Joey says.

Everyone immediately starts digging in their pockets for cash and they all run to the truck, stopping at the driveway. Laughing and joking as they purchase their treats, this group sounds like kids much younger than they are. With some kind of frozen treat in everyone's hands, they begin to open them as they make their way to the back yard. Sterling leads the way towards his gateway, but his concentration is on his ice cream instead of his prank. Just as he begins to walk through it, Kendra looks up and reads the sign aloud in a questioning tone. "Gateway to a magical summer evening?"

The words finally trigger Sterling's awareness, but it's too late; his body has already moved too far forward. With ice cream in his mouth and his eyes open in shock, cold water comes gushing out all around him, blasting his cone right out of his hand and soaking him from head to toe. The group is startled by the scene and they all jump backward, some falling into each other and knocking one or both kids to the ground. Sterling turns around in horror as everyone sees how he has been beaten by his own invention.

•••••••

"Oh my gosh, that was so funny," Allison comments as the story is concluded.

Nodding, Kendra agrees. "I know. Remember, I laughed so hard that ice cream squirted out of my nose?"

Everyone laughs as the story-telling continues.

"You guys are hilarious," Mr. Fisher says. "I've never seen a group that fits together so well."

"Yeah, I guess we really do a lot of things together," Sterling says, smiling with a faraway look in his eyes.

"Yeah, like all the costume parties," Raul says, smiling.

"Let's see, we've had so many costume parties. There was the Bible figures party, the seventies and eighties TV shows party..." Joey says.

"Oh yeah, Da Juan came as Venus Flytrap from *WKRP in Cincinnati*. Man, he looked just like him," Sterling adds.

Waving her arms back and forth, Allison interrupts. "Ooh, don't forget last year's condiment costume party."

"Yeah, you two show up as ketchup and mustard," Kendra adds, shaking her head.

"You do know that he specifically picked that theme so he could be mustard, right?" Sterling clarifies.

"No," Allison and Kendra say in unison. Quickly looking at each other, they then say, "Jinx," before rolling back into their chairs, laughing.

"Oh yeah, he just *had* to be mustard. The whole family just loves mustard," Sterling says.

"So? I like mustard. What's wrong with that?" Raul asks, puzzled.

"No, I don't mean like; I mean they are *crazy* about mustard. They put it on everything. I mean, seriously. It kinda makes me weirded out sometimes. I have to turn away."

The group begins laughing at him and telling him that he is overreacting.

"No, seriously. That's why his name is Da Juan," Sterling offers.

"The mustard is Dijon, Goofball," Allison quips.

"I know. I think they spelled it different to be coy. You know his cousin's name is Spicy, don't you?"

"Yeah, but that's just a nickname," Allison responds.

"No, it's not—and he has another cousin named Tre'. I call him Tree, though. You know, like a mustard tree. He never corrects me," Sterling says, nodding his head with his eyebrows raised.

Just then Mr. and Mrs. Noble arrive, and Spicy and Tre' are with them. Everyone bursts into laughter except Sterling, whose eyes are frozen like a deer in the headlights. As everyone greets them, they are interrupted by the doctor walking towards them.

Chapter Thirty

That's a lot of sticky notes

Two weeks later brings us back to today.
The sun shines as brightly as the mischievous smile on Sterling's face as he steps out of his car and closes the door. His familiar energetic stride seems effortless as he walks across the parking lot and into the office supply store. Cheerfully he greets everyone else in the store, both customers and employees. Down through the aisles he goes, searching for the just the right thing. He catches a glimpse of Allison out of the corner of his eye. She is straightening some file folders on the next aisle over. His grin is so wide his face can barely hold it all, and the gleam in his eyes can only mean one thing. Allison has seen this look before. With a quick glance back to see where the manager is, she walks hurriedly to catch up with him.

"What are you up to?" Allison says, in that tone your mother uses when she catches you doing something naughty.

"Good morning to you as well, Allison. Why, yes; it is a lovely day, and I am fine. Thank you so much for asking," Sterling responds in his usual confident voice as he comes to a stop in one of the aisles.

"Don't you try to use that stuff on *me*, Sterling. I know that look on your face. Now, what are you doing?"

"I'm just here in search of some much-needed office supplies, young worker lady, and yes, that would be very nice of you, to help me on my ever so important quest." Sterling says in as cheesy a manner as he possibly could.

"No, Sterling. No, I'm not helping you with this one," she replies, shaking her head and holding both hands out as she backs away a step. "It's too soon."

"It's never too soon for office supplies." He says as he leans in a little closer. "You do realize that your current line of work is predicated on your ability to help people find and purchase office supplies, don't you?"

Allison huffs at him and crosses her arms, shooting him a stare that would go right through him if eyes were weapons.

"What?" Sterling says as he shrugs his shoulders. "Ooh, here they are." He points to the sticky notes on the shelf, then begins to look around for a basket. "Hey, where are the baskets?"

She rolls her eyes at him then turns and walks away. He looks at another customer and smiles. "She is just a little testy today. I don't know why. It's a beautiful day, don't you think?" he says as he shrugs again. The lady just smiles back at him and shakes her head.

Allison walks back and holds her arm out, extending a basket to him as she comes to a quick and forceful stop beside him. "Here; now, *what are you up to?*" she demands, a bit louder than she meant to. Several other shoppers turn to see what is going on. Sterling starts putting packs of sticky notes in the basket, pulling them off the rack in handfuls. Allison, embarrassed, whispers. "Sterling, for the love of everything good and holy, what are you doing?"

Whispering in return, Sterling replies, "I told you, I'm simply getting office supplies." He pulls the last bunch off the rack and drops then in the basket. "Do you have any more in the back? I already wiped out all the other stores in town."

Now totally frustrated, she hisses back at him, "*What? No*, and one thing I have learned over the years is that nothing is ever simple when it comes to you."

"Oh, you're so sweet," Sterling retorts. He grabs her free hand and starts pulling her through the store. "Now, where are the markers?"

"Stop it! And let go of my hand," she fires back, jerking her hand free. "You're gonna get me fired."

"Here they are," he says cheerfully, as he picks a pack of markers off the hook. Tilting his head, he turns to Allison and asks, "Will these bleed through?"

Sighing and shaking her head, she takes the pack from him and looks at it for a second. Putting it back on the hook, she picks up a different pack. "Here, use these," she says, putting the new pack in the basket.

"Great!" he says, pulling the rest of that brand off the pegboard display, letting them fall into the basket.

"He needs more time, Sterling. It's only been a few days," she pleads.

"Trust me, Allison. This is exactly what he needs," Sterling says, much more serious now. "I haven't forgotten what we just went through. What *he* just went through. This is my best friend. My boy. My partner in cr—well, you know, not *crime*, but everything mischievous that is considered legal." Now Sterling is smiling again. "This is what I would want, and I know it's what he wants. He needs to get back to normal as soon as possible."

Next Summer

"OK," she concedes. "If you're sure about this... I hope you know what you're doing."

"Plus, how bad could it be? It's just sticky notes and markers. Ooh, I almost forgot: eight o'clock at my house. We have enough people, so it shouldn't take too long. See ya then, right?"

"Oh, no! I want nothing to do with this," She quickly replies, shaking her head and waving her hands back and forth in a warding-off gesture.

"Yeah yeah, whatever. I'll see ya then," Sterling confidently says, turning to leave.

Smiling and shaking her head, Allison whispers to herself, "Yeah, I'll see ya there."

•••••••

As all the group assembles for the first time since their trip and the horrifying bank ordeal, they all are wondering what Sterling is up to and what sticky notes could possibly have to do with it. Laughter fills the room as they sit and talk. There's no pressure, no more traveling, just being with each other. Sterling is next door at the Noble residence, preparing for his latest master plan. His parents let his friends in and watch as they once again make themselves at home, both in their house and with each other. With the mission trip now complete and the summer drawing to an end, this will be one of the last times the entire group will be together for a while. Some will be going off to college, others will be going to work, and still others will be doing some mixture of the two. Tonight, however, is for them all. It is a chance to work together once more, a time for fellowship. Another memory to cherish for a lifetime. Sterling's parents have offered snacks while they wait, and the adults sit in the kitchen watching and listening, thankful that tonight is another good night—just three days ago, so much was in danger.

Finally, Sterling bounces in through the front door to an array of hellos and cheers. In his hand is a box full of the tools he has gathered for his project. "Thanks guys, for coming to help tonight. I know that not everyone agrees with my madness," he says, nodding to Allison, "but trust me. We almost lost our leader. Thank God we did not. He will be home in a couple of hours, and I want to pull off a huge welcome home prank. A very bright, colorful, low-stress prank." Everyone begins to grin with anticipation as he continues. "I've been all over town and bought all the sticky note pads and markers I could find, and I need all of you to help me with his surprise. So, let's go!" He gets up and leads the way out the front door and across the yard to Da Juan's house.

•••••••

With the job complete and the expectation of Da Juan's arrival any moment, the group all gathers outside the Nobles' garage. Sterling, having texted Da Juan earlier, knows when to expect them home.

As the Noble's car pulls into the driveway, the whole group begins to jump up and down, cheering and clapping. Da Juan steps out of the driver's side rear passenger door and shuts it with his left hand. His right arm is in a sling, and will be for several weeks. He is still tired and a little weak, but very glad to be home. The smile on his face confirms that his friends have made it a very special moment. "I didn't expect you guys to be here," he says, "but I'm glad you are."

"That's what you call one of those *surprises*," Joey says walking up and giving him the first of many careful hugs as the rest of the group files in behind him.

"Well, we couldn't really have our last party of the summer without you, now could we?" Allison says.

"No, I guess not," he replies.

One by one, the whole group makes their way to him, hugging and welcoming him home as if they haven't seen him for years. Sterling brings up the rear, pulling him in for a hug. "I'm glad you're OK, Bro," he says.

"Thanks, Bro I really appreciate this party. I'm sure it was your idea," Da Juan replies.

"Well, don't thank me just yet."

Da Juan begins to look a little concerned as to what that means. "What ya up to, Bro?"

"Well. I wanted to have this little shindig to welcome you home, but you know how big I am on surprises and decorations," Sterling says, grinning widely.

"Surprise decorations, huh?" Da Juan replies, looking around a bit to see if he can figure out what's going on before it is revealed to him.

"Yeah, something like that," Kendra chuckles, patting him on his good shoulder.

"I hope it's not another gateway to a magical summer evening," Da Juan laughs as he says it, then grimaces at the pain in his shoulder.

"Touché but no," Sterling replies, eyebrows raised. His grin seems about to burst off his face.

Angels Jankiel, Haniel, and Thaniel stand nearby and watch the glad reunion taking place. "Would you two like to help me with Smyth, Eric, and Russell?" Jankiel asks.

"Absolutely. I think that's a wonderful idea," Haniel replies.

"Of course, but shh. They're about to reveal the surprise," Thaniel says.

"You already know what's in the garage, Thaniel," Haniel says.

"I know, but I want to see Da Juan's reaction. I can't press rewind like a DVR."

Jankiel begins to laugh. "Well, he has you there," he says.

"We wanted to leave you with some decorations to show you how happy we are that you are home and on the mend," Sterling says, leading Da Juan closer to the garage.

Grinning, he says, "So you decorated our garage? How thoughtful."

"Well—" Sterling begins to speak, but is interrupted.

"Wait a minute." Da Juan's face goes from grinning to very concerned in an instant. "Where is my car?"

Sterling nods to Raul, who clicks the button on the garage door remote. The door lifts slowly, revealing Da Juan's car, covered from bumper to bumper with hundreds of sticky notes. The group begins to cheer and clap again as Da Juan's eyes bug out at the multi-colored spectacle before him. Clapping his hands softly, since his right arm is in a sling, he walks around the car, smiling and taking it all in. The roof is covered in purple, the doors and fenders in blue. The wheels are green and the tires are white. The lights are covered in orange for the blinkers, and pink for the tail lights. The headlights and all the glass pieces are yellow, and the bumpers are a rainbow of them all. Eyes are drawn on the windshield with markers, and there's a smile drawn on the grill. Words of encouragement and congratulations cover the entire car. Da Juan gives out hugs and fist bumps as he circles the car. Speaking across the front end of the car, he calls out to Sterling. "So, it takes me getting shot in the shoulder to get everyone involved in a prank at the same time? That's messed up, Dude."

"I know, right?" Sterling replies with a smile. "This was the first time, wasn't it? You know, we figured that by the time you used that left hand to pick all of these off, your right shoulder should be healed."

As the earthly friends continue on with their fellowship around the car, the heavenly friends prepare to leave. Looking at each other, they all speak in unison. "Back to work? Yep." With that they all fly off.

Finally making his way back to Sterling, Da Juan gives him a nod, a fist bump, and a half hug, protecting his painful right shoulder. "Love you, Bro."

"Love you too, Bro."

Epilogue

Friendship, in forty-five thousand words or less

So, here we are back where we started. Friendship really is a wonderful thing. Not everyone has it on this grand a scale, I know. However, the strength given by a friend such as Jonathan can help a shepherd boy like David become a wise king. Proverbs 18:24 (KJV) says, "A man that hath friends must shew himself friendly: and there is a friend that sticketh closer than a brother." I began by telling you about my friends Da Juan and Sterling, and how they showed the rest of us how to be friends. They showed a confused young bank robber how to be a friend to a stranger. They showed a scared boy how to be a part of a group. They have been showing us for years how to bring joy and laughter to the ones you love, and how to not take yourself too seriously while taking your own actions very seriously.

So, this thing called friendship: What does it really mean? In scripture, the good Samaritan showed a man in need what being a friend is. The members of the early church in the New Testament gave of themselves to help their brothers and sisters in need. Even Jonah, who fought against God and was swallowed by a whale, finally learned what friendship is when he preached a message that God used to save a whole city. Of course, we can't forget God himself, who befriended us by sending his own son to take on flesh to be with us. And Jesus, who loved us enough to die in our place to make a way for our salvation. So, what is friendship? It's a helping hand. It's a meal to the hungry. It's simply being there for someone who is grieving. It's many things to many people, but when we do something to be a friend to someone else, we are blessed in return, somehow, someway. Scripture says what you sow you will also reap. We usually take that as a warning about our sin, but it also is a message of hope, when we are friends to others, God will send us friends as well.

I know you probably have questions, so here goes. Mr. and Mrs. Bishop believed that when they saw a feather, there was an angel close. Do I believe that? I don't know. I don't *not* believe it. There are too many questions in this life that I can't answer, and the Bible does speak of angels being here when we are unaware of them. So, could angels be helping us? Why not? What do they do? How do they do it? I don't know that either, but to think that a heavenly being is here watching me and trying to point me to God is a good thought. And if that's true, then Lord help me listen to them.

I haven't had a chance yet to ask Da Juan about the feather he found in the bank, but I plan to. Oh yeah, Da Juan is doing just fine, and so is Sterling. Still best buds, and goofy as ever. Now, that last week of our trip? Once Da Juan was in the clear, we went to the church and helped them. Everyone but Da Juan helped, of course, but we sent him videos of our progress.

Smyth, Eric, and Russell? They did all go to jail, but of course Smyth has the longest sentence. We do feel bad for them, and are praying for them. I hope they can turn their lives around and find the Lord.

Renee and Jason? Well, she and the baby are doing fine, and still on course for a healthy delivery. I'm sure Jason is good with that, and she forbade him to risk his life again. Renee has switched him to online banking.

Our teacher, Mr. Fisher? Well, he is preparing for his second graduating class. He couldn't possibly top us, though; could he?

Oh yeah, last but not least, how many sticky notes does it take to cover an entire car? Well, I can tell you, it's more than a few. Sterling bought 120 packs, and we had less than a pack left over once the car was covered. Naturally, that blew my mind, so I asked Sterling how he was able to get that close. His answer? He told me he did the math, and math is your friend—and friends are everything.

About the Author

Dale P. Rhodes, Sr. was born in central Virginia and still lives there today. He wrote poetry and short stories in high school. After graduation life became centered around work, bills, and parenthood and writing was pushed to the back burner.

The death of Dale's father stirred his pen to life again. Dale's first book, *Daddy's Apple Tree*, is a tribute to his father, mother, and many of the moments that shaped his life.

During the summer of 2014 Dale had the strong impression that he should write a story about a guardian angel. After days of prayer, he was overwhelmed with a story that came faster than he could write it down. *If Only* is the culmination of that experience, a story of a guardian angel who feels like he has failed mankind and the trials that have shaped him for hundreds of years.

Dale's third book, entitled *Next Summer*, is the story of an epic friendship between two boys that lead their senior class on the trip of a lifetime. From five years old to graduation, these boys create a bond with everyone they meet. It was inspired by a co-worker who is so friendly that he has seemingly never met a stranger.

Dale loves his wife and their four grown children. He also loves movies, music, sports, and doing projects around the house. His rescue dogs and cats are his babies now. Dale continues to write and hopes to have his fourth and fifth books coming to fruition in the near future.

CPSIA information can be obtained
at www.ICGtesting.com
Printed in the USA
FSHW04n2200110418
46622FS